The only lucky one

THE COLONY:
RENEGADES

#1 Bestseller
Michaelbrent
COLLINGS

Book Two of the Colony Saga

For more information on Michaelbrent's books, including specials and sales; and for info about signings, appearances, and media,

check out his webpage,

"Like" his Facebook fanpage
or
Follow him on Twitter.

PRAISE FOR THE NOVELS OF
MICHAELBRENT COLLINGS

THE COLONY: GENESIS (THE COLONY, VOL. 1)

"Once again Michaelbrent delivers a smashing novel with *The Colony: Genesis*, the first book in a proposed new series. From start to finish, this novel is a fresh look into the world of apocalyptic proportions, brought on by anyone's guess.... the action and intrigue throughout is almost non-stop. I read it in less than two days, and I'm glad I did." *- Horror Drive-In*

"5 out of 5 stars.... I couldn't put it down." *- Media Mikes*

"If you love Zombie stories, you will love The Colony. If you are a so-so fan of Zombie stories, you will love The Colony and if you love good horror, written well and told in a way that you will lose a night's sleep because you do not want to stop reading, you will definitely love The Colony." *– Only Five Star Book Reviews*

"I barely had time to buckle my mental seatbelt before the pedal hit the metal...." *– The Horror Fiction Review*

"What a refreshing read. This is the first of a series and if this is any indication of what's to come, count me in! .... If I could, I would gladly give this novel a 10 star rating." *– Horror Novel Reviews*

STRANGERS

"Highly recommended." *– Hellnotes*

"Collings is so proficient at what he does, he crooks his finger to get you inside his world and before you know it, you are along for the ride. You don't even see it coming; he is that good." *– Only Five Star Book Reviews*

"Move over Stephen King... Clive Barker.... Michaelbrent Collings is taking over as the new king of the horror book genre." – *Media Mikes*

"*STRANGERS* is another white-knuckled journey that demands to be read in one sitting." – *The Horror Fiction Review*

"Michaelbrent spins a tale that keeps you enthralled from page to page.... Overall I give this novel an A." – *The Horror Drive-In*

DARKBOUND

"Really good, highly recommended, make sure you have time to read a lot at one sitting since you may have a hard time putting it down." – *The Horror Fiction Review*

"In *Darkbound* you will find the intensity of *Misery* and a journey reminiscent of the train ride in *The Talisman*.... A proficient and pedagogical author, Collings' works should be studied to see what makes his writing resonate with such vividness of detail.... You will not be disappointed in this dark tale." – *Hellnotes*

"*Darkbound* travels along at a screaming pace with action the whole way through, and twists to keep you guessing throughout.... With an ending that I didn't see coming from a mile away, and easily one of the best I've had the enjoyment of reading in a long time...." – *Horror Drive-In*

THE HAUNTED

"*The Haunted* is a terrific read with some great scares and a shock of an ending!" – Rick Hautala, international bestselling author; Bram Stoker Award® for Lifetime Achievement winner

"[G]ritty, compelling and will leave you on the edge of your seat.... *The Haunted* is a tremendous read for fans of ghoulishly good terror." – horrornews.net

"*The Haunted* is just about perfect.... This is a haunted house story that will scare even the most jaded horror hounds. I loved it!" – Joe McKinney, Bram Stoker Award®-winning author of *Flesh Eaters* and *Inheritance*

APPARITION

"*Apparition* is not just a 'recommended' novel, it is easily one of the most entertaining and satisfying horror novels this reviewer has read within the past few years. I cannot imagine that any prospective reader looking for a new read in the horror genre won't be similarly blown away by the novel." – *Hellnotes*

"[*Apparition* is] a gripping, pulse hammering journey that refuses to relent until the very final act. The conclusion that unfolds may cause you to sleep with the lights on for a spell.... Yet be forewarned perhaps it is best reserved for day time reading." – horrornews.net

"*Apparition* is a hard core supernatural horror novel that is going to scare the hell out of you.... This book has everything that you would want in a horror novel.... it is a roller coaster ride right up to a shocking ending." – horroraddicts.net

"[*Apparition* is] Riveting. Captivating. Mesmerizing.... [A]n effective, emotional, nerve-twisting read, another amazingly well-written one from a top-notch writer." – *The Horror Fiction Review*

THE LOON

"It's always so nice to find one where hardcore asylum-crazy is done RIGHT.... *THE LOON* is, hands down, an excellent book." – *The Horror Fiction Review*

"Highly recommended for horror and thriller lovers. It's fast-moving, as it has to be, and bloody and violent, but not disgustingly gory.... Collings knows how to write thrillers, and I'm looking forward to reading more from him." – *Hellnotes*

MR. GRAY (AKA THE MERIDIANS)

"... an outstanding read.... This story is layered with mystery, questions from every corner and no answers fully coming forth until the final conclusion.... What a ride.... This is one you will not be able to put down and one you will remember for a long time to come. Very highly recommended." – *Midwest Book Review*

HOOKED: A TRUE FAERIE TALE

"*Hooked* is a story with depth.... Emotional, sad, horrific, and thought provoking, this one was difficult to put down and now, one of my favourite tales." – *Only Five Star Book Reviews*

"[A]n interesting and compelling read.... Collings has a way with words that pulls you into every moment of the story, absorbing every scene with all of your senses." – *Clean Romance Reviews*

"Collings has found a way to craft an entirely new modern vampire mythology – and one strikingly different from everything I've seen before.... Recommended for adult and teen fans of horror and paranormal romance...." – *Hellnotes*

RISING FEARS

"The writing is superb. The characters are believable and sympathetic... the theme of a parent who's lost a child figures strongly; it's powerful stuff, and written from the perspective of experience that no one should ever have to suffer." – *The Horror Fiction Review*

DEDICATION

To...

Chad Brown (VAWCF)...

and to Laura, FTAAE.

Contents

1

The world had ended four hours ago.

So why was Kenny G still playing music?

Ken Strickland knew he was asking this question as a way to avoid the *real* questions, the questions he *should* be asking. The questions that had no answers.

But still, it seemed so important.

Civilization had fallen. Zombies had taken over. Zombies whose bites caused instant conversion, who were impervious to pain or grief or discomfort. Monsters whose only apparent thought seemed to be focused on killing those few normal humans that remained.

But Kenny G was still playing music.

Ken Strickland had never hated Kenny G before. Never particularly liked him, but didn't *hate* him. Now, though, in an elevator in the Wells Fargo Center, riding up toward the ninth floor where he hoped against all reason to find his wife and three children alive, he realized that the fall of civilization came with some perks.

There would be no more easy listening, no more Muzak.

Beside him, Dorcas shuffled nervously. The middle-aged woman was tough as weathered saddle leather. She had saved Ken's life several times, even though he was a virtual stranger to her. But she was nervous now, traveling up in a confined space with nowhere to run, nowhere to hide if things went bad.

Maybe we should have taken the stairs.

He discarded that idea almost instantly. Stairs would have taken too long. And the last time they had used the stairs, things had gone badly.

Plus, who knew how long the power would last? This might be the last trip any of them would ever take in an elevator. This might be a magical moment they would tell children and grandchildren about someday.

If we live that long.

"Wonder how many times people took this elevator," said Christopher. The twenty-two year old looked wistful, as though thinking along the same lines as Ken. He had been the son of Idaho's governor until a few hours ago. Then, like all of the people in the elevator, he became just one more survivor, one more refugee, one more person fleeing the hordes that had taken over the world in less than ten minutes.

Aaron grunted. Ken couldn't tell if the cowboy was agreeing with Christopher, or telling him to be quiet. The older man was the most enigmatic of the group. Ken wondered anew who he was. How he'd learned to fight, how the older man seemed to know what to do in almost any situation.

Mysteries. Mysteries in mysteries in mysteries.

No one knew anything anymore.

Welcome to the new world.

The counter on the front panel of the elevator dinged at each floor, a low electronic chirp that was designed to be pleasing and unobtrusive. Each twitter set Ken's teeth on edge, made him want to tear the circuitry out by its roots in order to shut down the sound.

4 (ding)… 5 (ding)… 6 (ding)….

Dorcas' hand tightened against Ken's right arm. The hand that held him was strong, though her other hand hung from the end of a makeshift sling, broken during a zombie attack. Aaron had a handful of broken fingers and a dislocated thumb. Ken had had to cut off the pinkie and ring fingers of his own hand in order to escape an attack.

Everyone was injured. Broken. Beaten down.

7 (ding)….

Only Christopher looked fine. Better than fine. He looked like a cover model, stopped for a latte break and helping out with the zombie apocalypse for a few minutes until the photographer called him back on set.

8 (ding)….

"Get ready," said Aaron.

Christopher nodded. Ken did, too, though he wondered what they would do to get ready. Aaron had a gun, but it only had two bullets. Other than that the party was weaponless. And even if they each had an assault rifle and full body armor, Ken didn't know what that would do against hordes of seemingly indestructible attackers. Nothing seemed to stop the things. Even major head trauma didn't slow them down; just sent them into an indiscriminate rage that would have them attacking anything that moved – including each other.

The elevator dinged. The final floor.

Ken closed his eyes for a moment. He said a silent prayer. Imagined Maggie's face. The smiles of Derek, Hope, and Liz.

Please let them be alive. Or let them be dead.

Just not things. Not zombies.

The elevator doors opened.

2

The elevator opened to a corridor. Just a blank wall. Normal, save only for the thick smear of brown-red-black that trailed down its middle.

Christopher stepped forward, clearly intending to move into the hallway. Aaron grabbed him.

"Stop," the cowboy said. It was barely a whisper. The kind of speech Ken associated with survival.

Christopher halted. The four people in the elevator were silent. Ken couldn't even hear anyone breathing. They were held in a momentary stasis, an instant before the future hit them with its usual freight-train momentum.

What if Maggie's gone? The kids?

"Okay," breathed the cowboy.

Christopher stepped out of the elevator cab.

He looked to his left and right, and Ken saw him grow pale.

"What?" said Ken.

Christopher turned around. Fast. Like he didn't want Ken coming out.

"Maybe you shouldn't –" he began.

Ken stepped out of the elevator.

And felt a scream tear loose from his throat.

3

Aaron's good hand clamped over Ken's mouth, stopping the scream before more than a whimper came out. Then the cowboy leaned over and retched. None of them had eaten since this all started, since the world ended. There was nothing in the man's stomach. But he dry-heaved as though his body was trying to expel the very memory of what he was seeing at either end of the corridor, only about twenty feet away from the elevators.

Two solid walls. Not of brick and mortar, not of plaster or wood.

Bodies.

It looked like every single person on this floor had run for the elevator at the same time. And every single person had fallen prey to whatever had turned the world upside down.

The hall was blocked at either end by a solid plug of corpses, bodies and body parts ripped limb from limb and then piled atop each other haphazardly like a madman's version of an Erector set. Heads, arms, legs, trunks. Entire bodies shredded and then stuffed into place.

"What...?" Dorcas' voice was soft. So soft, like the vision of death in the still-lit corridor had somehow stolen away the very years she had lived. Had turned her into a little girl, shying away from thunder and whimpering at the vision of lightning in the sky.

Humanity's defenses had been stripped off. All pretenses of civilization pulled away, and not even their dead were sacrosanct. Even humanity's holiest objects had been rendered profane. The monsters had come for them.

"What do we do?" said Christopher.

No one spoke. The lights above them flickered, and Ken wondered what would happen if the lights failed – as they would have to do eventually – while they were stuck here between the bodies of the dead.

He was shaking. His head ached, his back hurt where he had twisted it earlier, the bones of his left leg felt like white-hot pincers were clamped against them every few inches.

His absent fingers, the ones he had hacked off himself, ached. He missed his wedding ring.

He walked toward the wall of bodies on his right.

He reached out and grabbed a stiff hand. Pulled it away from the wall of the dead.

A moment later Dorcas and Christopher joined him and they started to dig through the bodies.

Aaron waited a moment. He had been standing halfway in the elevator cab, and now he looked around and spotted something in the hall: a small aluminum trash can. He stomped it flat, then wedged it in the track of the elevator. Ken saw Christopher eyeing the older man.

"We don't want anything surprising us from behind," said the cowboy. "And better to have the elevator available when we want it."

Christopher nodded and resumed digging.

They pulled bodies and dismembered bits away. Piled them along the corners of the hall. Ken tried very hard not to think about what he was doing. And failed miserably.

He wondered what he would do if one of the hands he touched turned out to be small. Soft. The hand of a child. A hand he recognized.

He kept digging.

4

Slow going.

It was harder than Ken would have thought. Partly because it was just emotionally taxing to grab ahold of a piece of what had once been a *person*, to pull it out of a pile of other pieces. To drag it behind you and try not to think of what you were doing, of the reality of what was happening.

Part of it was because everyone stopped every minute or so. Just stopped as one, no words spoken. Listening. Trying to hear the sound of thunder that would indicate one of the hordes of thousands of once-human killers that now ruled the world. Or perhaps listening for the growl, that otherworldly sound that the things made. As a single voice it was disquieting, a sound like someone gargling a mixture of gravel and razor blades. In a large chorus it had a strange power, a psychic effect that encouraged you to just give up, to give in and die.

But there was also something else at work. Something making their job more difficult. At first Ken thought it was his imagination, this last obstacle – a literal wall of gore between him and a goal that he didn't even know for sure still existed – just pushing him over the edge and making everything seem harder than it really was.

Until Dorcas grunted. "What the...?" she said. As with all words in this place that was bookended by death, the words were whispered. And as with all the words thus far, even whispered they seemed far too loud. Ken felt like they were screaming in a church. Any life here had become an obscenity.

The dead ruled this place. The living were interlopers. Were profane.

"What is it?" said Christopher. Even his ever-present smile had waned in the gory environment, though he had somehow managed to keep his clothing less spattered with filth than should be possible.

Dorcas hesitated. Then she held out the piece of former humanity – now reduced to so much ghastly masonry – that she had yanked out of the crumbling wall of death. "What is this stuff?" she said.

The others moved closer. Ken wanted to keep pulling at the bodies at this end of the corridor. He knew that taking a break was a bad idea; that if he stopped, getting started again would be that much harder.

But he *did* stop. He looked with the rest.

Dorcas was holding an arm. It looked like it had once belonged to a woman. The long, elegant arm of a woman in her twenties or thirties. Thin and beautiful. Fingers with several rings. Arm covered in a once-tailored suit sleeve that had been shredded.

The shoulder ended in a stump. It glistened. But not with blood. A pus-yellow substance coated the end of the arm, the flickering lights above them reflecting dully off the waxy patina.

Christopher reached out to touch it. Aaron stopped him. Grabbed the kid's hand. "Don't," said the cowboy.

"What?" said Christopher. "It might be important."

"So you're just going to stick your finger in it?" said Aaron. "You remember that thing that puked acid before we came up here?"

Christopher stopped. But only for a moment. Then he poked the yellow substance. Dorcas yipped in sympathy, as though expecting his finger to melt off.

Christopher grinned. "Nothing ventured." He removed his finger, touching it with his thumb. "Tacky," he said. "Feels like...." He searched for the words. "Wet Play-Doh?"

"What do you think it's for?" asked Dorcas.

Aaron shrugged. The older man turned around and grabbed the next piece of the wall of body parts. Another hand.

And he screamed, a strange scream that he bit off, muffled it the way they were all learning to do, the way they were learning they *had* to do in order to survive.

But the rest of the survivors heard.

They turned.

Ken saw what had scared the normally imperturbable cowboy.

Saw the hand that Aaron had grabbed.

The hand that was *moving*.

5

Ken stumbled back from the movement, falling into Dorcas and Christopher even as Aaron backpedaled as well.

And what remained of the wall of the dead collapsed.

There was a crackling sound that reminded Ken of ice crunching underfoot on a winter day, and then the bodies that had been so hard to pull apart only a moment ago just seemed to... *drift* like so many snowflakes caught in a windstorm.

All that was left was the hand. Still moving. Attached to a middle-aged man who stood in the place just beyond the wall. The man was dressed in the ragged remains of a gray business suit. Expensive-looking glasses hung askew from his blue face.

His chest and arms were coated in the waxy substance that Dorcas had just found.

He looked at the survivors. And even without seeing the bite marks that seemed to glow like brands along his neck and the right part of his jaw, Ken would have been able to tell from the look in the thing's eyes.

It wasn't a man at all. Not anymore.

The four survivors froze. Running for the elevator was out of the question: even if they got inside, there was no way they could get the doors closed and get the thing moving before the zombie was on them. And a single bite would end the struggle.

"Think we can take it?" whispered Christopher. Ken didn't look, but suspected the kid was still smiling. Only this would be a death-grin, the kind of smile worn by a man about to kill or be killed.

"Let's hope so," said Aaron. "There's just one."

The thing in the suit held up its arms. It made a strange sound. Not the growl that Ken was used to. More of a cross between a dentist's drill and something you might hear during a recording of exotic birds. Loud and thoroughly unpleasant.

An instant later, ten more of the things shuffled into the hall.

6

All of them pushed into the corridor, the flickering lights making them appear at once ghostly and all-too-solid. Six men and four women joined the original business-suited thing.

They all made that same strange chirping.

Dorcas started whimpering. A noise that Ken didn't expect from her, not from the woman who had saved his butt repeatedly. But then, she'd never been pushed up against a wall of corpses, facing certain death – or worse – like this.

The things stepped toward them. As with other groups of the things, these moved in a coordinated fashion. Not lockstep or synchronized, but they never bumped into each other either. They seemed to be aware on some level beyond sight or sound where each of their fellows were and would be.

Aaron pulled out his gun. A .357 Magnum with two bullets. The draw was a bit awkward since he had to pull it with his left hand and it was set for a right-handed draw.

Aaron looked at Ken, and Ken saw in his eyes the question: "Are you brave enough to face them?"

Ken nodded minutely. He knew what the cowboy was saying, what he was asking.

Aaron turned to Dorcas. He smiled to her. "Don't worry," he said. His voice was soft. Not just quiet, but soft. The cowboy sounded like a father saying good night to a sick child. Like a husband saying goodbye to a beloved wife.

He clicked back the hammer.

Dorcas pulled her gaze away from the approaching beasts long enough to see what Aaron had in his hands. To see what he had in his mind.

Ken saw her shake her head.

Then the motion turned to a nod. Acceptance. Better to die than to become one of the things.

Aaron pointed the gun at her.

Ken wondered who would get the last of the two remaining bullets. He supposed it would be Christopher. He thought that was what Aaron's look had meant: an old-fashioned request to let the women and children go free. Even if the children were simply the young men, and the only freedom available was the promise of quick death.

Dorcas closed her eyes. A trace of a smile played along her lips. She looked at peace.

Aaron's trigger finger clenched.

7

"Wait!"

The voice spun Ken around like a top. He expected to hear the deafening blast of Aaron's gun discharging, the sound of Dorcas' brains exploding through the already-defiled hallway.

But there was nothing. No sound. Aaron must have caught himself. Waited on Christopher's shouted word.

One of the things had reached the kid. It had leaned in. Its teeth were chittering, snapping as though attacking the air itself. Christopher held so still he almost appeared to be a statue.

The zombie before him – a woman in a skirt and blouse that were so bright red they seemed offensively out of place – leaned in even closer.

And did not bite him.

She bent over. Picked up a dismembered leg. She coughed. The last time Ken had heard that ugly, gagging cough, the zombie doing it had vomited a black acid that had melted concrete. He tensed, waiting for Christopher to be splashed with the tarry substance, waiting for the young man to start screaming.

It didn't happen.

Instead, the red-garbed monster vomited up a slick yellow substance. Ken realized that the thing had it all over the front of her clothes. Just like the first one they had found in the corridor. And, he saw, just like the other zombies that had crowded into this space.

The woman rubbed the end of the leg in the yellowy bile and then lay it on the floor before turning away, looking for another gory building block.

Ken realized that the yellow was some kind of biological mortar.

The things were *building*.

But what?

And why weren't they attacking him and his friends?

"We should go," said Christopher.

Ken was torn. He needed to find his family.

But there was bravery… and there was suicide.

He turned back to the elevator. Dorcas turned with him. They both stepped together, as synchronized as the monsters all around them.

And the zombies growled.

Ken froze. He looked behind him. The original monster, the one in the gray suit, was now staring right at him and Dorcas. Eyes looking at and through them both. Madness and rage battling for supremacy in its gaze. Ken waited for it to attack.

A moment later, it returned its gaze to the body it was trying to pull back into place.

Ken took another step toward the elevator.

Another growl. He looked back again. This time it wasn't just the gray-suited zombie, but more than half of the things that had crammed their way into the hall.

"I don't think they want us to leave," said Christopher.

8

Christopher waved, gesturing for the others to follow him as he began walking down the corridor, threading his way between the eleven zombies that were now hiccupping and puking that waxy substance all over the place, using it as an adhesive to begin rebuilding the wall that Ken and the others had torn down.

After walking a few feet, Ken realized that the beasts had shifted subtly. Before, they had been simply working to rebuild the wall of corpses. They were still doing so, but had moved down the hall toward the elevator. Building so the wall would be between the survivors and the elevator.

Cutting them off.

Ken caught Dorcas' eye. Her jaw was clenched. No longer whimpering, back under control like the tough farm girl he had always taken her to be, but clearly unhappy about this new development.

The things kept working. Every so often one of them would make that weird chirping sound. Ken couldn't tell if it was an unconscious noise or a communication.

Then the beasts all stopped moving.

The survivors halted as well, as though their muscles had been intertwined with those of the beasts in the hallway.

The zombies raised their faces heavenward. Their mouths opened and they started breathing in time, panting.

In-out-in-out-in-out....

Ken had seen this, too. Each time it got shorter. Like a countdown.

This time the pause barely lasted ten seconds. And when it was over something different happened. Something new. And new was always bad.

The zombies shook their heads. Not like a person might do upon waking from a pleasant nap. No, they whipped their heads back and forth so violently it was like they were trying to shake their skulls free. Several of them started slamming their faces into the nearest walls, hitting so hard that the brittle crunch of breaking bones could be heard.

Ken braced for the madness that came whenever one of the beasts suffered head injury. It didn't come. The things all stopped moving again. Simultaneously. Completely. Ken wondered if the things everywhere in the city, the state – the *world* – were similarly silent.

Then they moved. They went back to rebuilding their structure of bodies as though nothing had happened, vomiting up the glue-like substance and sticking pieces of what had once been people together in a wall that crept ever higher.

"I don't think we should be here when they finish," said Aaron.

"Yeah," said Christopher.

They walked the rest of the way down the hall. It ended in a T-intersection, allowing them to move to the right or the left.

"Which way?" said Dorcas.

Ken looked around. He didn't know.

Then he heard the scream.

9

There is no way to explain some things. No way to explain what it feels like to hold a new baby in your arms. No way to explain the joy of a new life.

There is also no way to explain the ache that takes hold of your heart when you hear one of your children cry in pain.

Derek broke his elbow when he was five. Nothing critical, just the typical little kid things that happen to everyone. Just a wrong move on a new bicycle. A moment in time that divided perfection from pain. One moment he was smiling, the next he was screaming.

Ken was home. It was summer. He saw it happen, and all he could think when it happened was how much he wished he had been working. Because the look on his boy's face was too much to bear. The look of pain – of real pain for the first time – coupled with the unspoken question, "Daddy, why did this happen? Why did you *let* this happen?"

Ken would rather have broken his own elbow than suffered through that moment for another instant.

Derek forgot about it. He was up riding his bike again the next day, trundling along in a bright purple cast that he seemed to pick precisely because it clashed with his red bike helmet. But Ken didn't forget. That scream became something that he heard in his dreams. The thing that signified the dangers of parenthood, the moments when you found that your children were vulnerable to the world.

It was that scream that told Ken that his children were as mortal as he. That they could be hurt. Could be killed.

It was the scream he heard now.

He ran to the right. The others pounded down the hall after him, but he was in the lead. And that was right. It was the way it had to be.

He had to get there first.

He was the daddy.

There were doors on either side of the hall. Some were closed, others were open. A few were missing: ripped off their moorings by hands far more powerful than they should have been. Blood stained the walls, but there were no bodies anywhere: all the corpses seemed to have been moved to the area near the elevators.

Ken ran past everything. The scream didn't repeat, but he ran without question for the door at the end of the hall. It had to be that one.

That was the one that was sealed. Not by locks or bolts.

No, it was covered by a thick curtain of that same tacky secretion. That yellow wax that the things in the halls were using.

Another scream.

Ken's child. Alive. Beyond the door.

And in pain.

10

Ken's own injuries and agonies disappeared.

There was nothing but the sound.

Before, when the zombies had come together in masses, their growls had made him and the others want to lay down and quit. To give up and die. He had thought that was the most devastating thing he would ever hear.

He was wrong.

The high-pitched trill of Derek's scream was worse. The scream of a little boy *in extremis* tore Ken's own aches and pains away in an instant. He bounded down the hall and was at the doorway full seconds ahead of the others. Pounding against the waxy substance with his hands, even the handkerchief-bound hand that ended in three fingers instead of five. Slamming at the tacky, glue-like secretion all over the door.

He left red streaks behind. He knew he should feel it, should feel the pain of one more attack against an already overburdened system. But he felt nothing.

"Derek!" he screamed.

"Daddy!" The call came back even higher than before. As though hearing his father's voice had not provided peace, but rather an increase of terror.

"I'm coming! I'm coming!"

But he didn't know that. He couldn't get a purchase on the slick wall of waxy mucus left behind by the monsters that had God-knew-what planned for his children.

Whump.

Something slammed into the substance beside Ken's head. He looked over as it was drawn back.

It was Christopher. The kid had found a tall, cylindrical trash can somewhere and was ramming it into the yellowish wall. Pieces of the secretion came off in flakes, then chunks, then sheets.

"Shit."

The word was whispered, but intense. Intense enough that it even managed to pull a grief- and terror-stricken father away from his single-minded task, if only for a moment.

Ken looked over his shoulder.

Whump. Whump. Whump. Christopher kept driving the trash can into the yellowed wall. A door began to emerge. Solid-looking, save for the glass window on the top where the words "Law Firm of Stacy Gomberg, Attorney At Law" could be vaguely made out, stenciled in gold lettering.

Whump. Whump.

Aaron and Dorcas had turned around. Facing behind them down the hall. Aaron still had his gun drawn, and had pulled the woman behind him in a gesture – useless – of protection.

The hall beyond the two was choked with zombies. All of them emitting that bizarre trill.

And walking toward them.

"Daddy!" screamed Derek from beyond the door. "Daddy, Mommy won't wake up!"

11

Before, the things in the hall had seemed almost unaware of the survivors. Focused solely on rebuilding their wall of bodies, on the grisly task of shutting off this part of the building.

Now, though, all of them were clearly staring at Ken and his friends. The madness was there, the rage simmering behind half-shuttered eyes. Something held them in check, but he didn't know what it was, or how long they would refrain from attacking.

And it didn't matter. There had to be more than thirty of the things crowded into the hall just a few feet beyond Aaron and Dorcas. No escape if they attacked.

"Daddy!"

"I'm coming!"

Ken turned back to the door. Peeling back immense shards of the substance that the things had vomited forth. Yanking it away from the door like half-dried plaster. Some of it stuck to his fingers, gummed up under his nails, and he wondered if he would ever be able to scrub his hands hard enough or long enough to make them feel clean again. He suspected not.

He also wondered if the stuff could be toxic. It had to be getting into his bloodstream, through the still seeping stumps at the end of his left hand. What if it infected him?

What if he changed?

The thought was enough to make him pause for a second. But only a second. Only long enough to think of the few people he had seen bitten. They had changed instantly. Human one second, and something terribly different – both more and less – in the next.

So no. He wasn't infected. He believed that. He *had* to believe that.

And there's nothing I can do about it at this point.

He pulled away another flaky, leprous mass of the resin.

Behind it was the doorknob.

He touched it.

The trilling of the creatures behind him went up in volume. Expectant. Excited.

Hungry.

"Daddy?"

His boy's voice sounded weaker. Terrified, anxious. Giving up.

Ken turned the knob.

12

Ken went to South America with his church group one summer. They visited six different countries in three months, twenty teenagers out to do good and three church leaders who – looking back – Ken was certain were mostly hoping no one died or ended up pregnant. Because sometimes achieving goodness ran a close second to the basic necessities of civilization.

Ken understood the trip was a great success. Houses were built. Wells were dug. Some lives were genuinely changed.

The things Ken mostly remembered, though, were the amazing case of diarrhea he picked up in Brazil, and the spiders that almost picked *him* up in Paraguay.

Paraguay, he understood from his reading, was basically a nothing place. The only landlocked country in South America. Lots of poverty. It had once been a technological and economic power of South America, and had even boasted the first steam-powered locomotive. But decades of political mismanagement had crushed the economy and the people, and over a century later that locomotive was still in use as basic transportation while other countries in South America were using diesel and electric trains.

Still, that made it perfect for a charity trip. Many people were in need. And a hundred dollars could feed a family for a month.

Ken went in with his friends. They built, they dug, they sweated in the hundred-degree-plus heat. They cowered from torrential rainstorms that came out of nowhere and disappeared just as fast as they had come.

And Ken made the mistake of going for a quick walk.

He just wanted to see what was in the foliage. Something had moved. He thought it might be a monkey – he had a strange desire to see a wild monkey – and followed the movement into the thick trees.

A moment later the sounds of his friends faded. He barely noticed. He was too entranced by the new world in which he had found himself.

It was sunset. The pinkest light he had ever seen picked its way through broad leaves, piercing air so thick and wet it felt like he was swimming all the time. He watched it set, not realizing he was walking toward it, not realizing he was following the setting sun like it was some sort of will-o'-the-wisp.

And then the spider dropped into view.

Not a big one. Just a small thing, the size of Ken's thumbnail, dark brown and curling around a filament that extended up into nothing. But it was followed by another.

And another.

And another.

Ken looked around. He saw more of the spiders. Hundreds. Thousands. *Millions.*

He had somehow wandered into a web of a size greater than anything he had ever heard of. It had to be thirty feet long, thirty feet high, thirty feet deep. And every inch or two was another spider.

They seemed to be swarming toward him.

Ken screamed. He dropped to his belly and did his best army crawl back the way he had come. Shrieking back into the area where his friends were taking a Coke break and talking about quitting for the night.

They laughed at his story. Until *they* saw the web. Then they stopped laughing.

Their local guide shrugged. He mumbled something in the local dialect, then told them in halting English that Ken was in no danger, the spiders made "happy tents" but left people alone.

Ken did not believe him. He dreamed of spiders for weeks.

But he never thought he would see a web like it again. Certainly not in the middle of a high-rise in downtown Boise.

He stepped into the room. Silken strands brushed against his arm.

"Good hell," said Christopher. Ken didn't look, but he was fairly sure the kid was referring to what was in front of them.

"Oh, shit," said Dorcas. Ken didn't look at her, either, but he was fairly sure *she* was talking about what was behind them.

The zombies in the hall stopped trilling. They started growling.

13

"RUN!" Aaron shouted.

Ken turned in time to see Dorcas and Aaron racing the last few yards to the attorney's office. Screaming in terror. The three dozen monsters behind. Aaron was pushing Dorcas, propelling her forward, faster, faster.

They ran into the room with Ken and Christopher.

And everything stopped.

Ken and Christopher were already motionless, held in a kind of mental stasis by what they had found in the room. Aaron and Dorcas seemed to be affected equally, halting only inches into the new area.

And the zombies....

They stopped just outside the doorway. Still snarling, still growling that awful growl.

One of them – the very same gray-suited thing that Ken and the others had first run into – reached out. Ken felt like his skin was covered in ants, like it was trying to separate from his muscles and bones and leap to one side. But he still couldn't move.

Not with what was behind him.

And his son... Derek was silent.

The zombie reached out.

Reached out... and grabbed the door. Swung it shut. The lettering "Law Firm of Stacy Gomberg, Attorney At Law" – now backwards – could be seen once more. So could dozens of shapes, dark forms leaning close.

One of the things – probably Gray-Suit – leaned in. Even through the door, the sound of the gagging cough was enough to make Ken wish he was deaf. The thing vomited, and something splashed against Stacy Gomberg, Esq.'s, office door.

More of the things clustered around the door. All of them gagging, coughing. Excreting.

"They're sealing us in," said Dorcas.

"Good times," said Christopher.

Ken turned away from them both. Because he heard Derek again.

Somewhere in the office.

Somewhere in the web.

Crying.

14

It was like looking for a dark ghost. Not only because the sound was so weak and faraway, but because it came from the depths of the gray-white-black masses of webbing that coated everything in the office.

The office itself was fairly large; apparently Stacy Gomberg ran a successful firm. There was a receptionist desk, a waiting area with chairs, an open central space with several doors leading to other offices.

At least, Ken thought that was the layout. The silken threads that covered everything made the most basic observations little more than blind guesses.

Even the air was spun thick with threads, with strands that stretched from ceiling to floor, from wall to wall. Ken saw the overhead fluorescent lights straining to illuminate the area, but the webbing seemed to be bouncing the photons back, rejecting the light itself. The office was dingy, dark. It felt like a prison. A dungeon. An oubliette on the ninth floor of a skyscraper.

Christopher shouted. Ken looked over. The younger man had stepped forward into the waiting area, and tripped over what looked like a thick mound of silk. The webbing had sheared apart, though, revealing a white face. Not a mound of silk, but a wrapped-over body.

Something hissed. This time it was Aaron who screamed, the cowboy permitting a rare showing of emotion as something moved behind him. What had been wall a moment before now shifted.

Not wall. Not wall at all.

It was a zombie. Encased in silk, spun into a cocoon-like shell. Standing silently right behind Aaron. Now it tore forth, ripping out of the threads that held it.

It went to the body that Christopher had revealed. Leaned over. Tore into its cheek and began to feed on it.

"Daddy, please help!"

Ken turned away. For whatever reason, the zombie wasn't bothering them. He had a child calling him.

One thing at a time.

He walked through the lobby area, shivering as the trails of silky material trailed over his bare skin. He felt like vomiting.

"Derek," he shouted, trying to keep his voice calm. Strong. And failing. "Where are you?"

"In here," said the voice.

Ken followed his son's voice. Derek still sounded hurt. And in this world where so many new kinds of pain had recently erupted into being, Ken hesitated to think of what that might mean.

He passed several offices. Barely glanced into them. Still, it was enough to show him nightmare visions, silk-wrapped sheets of once-life. Bulky objects that were once desks and bookshelves and filing cabinets and phones and people.

Some of the corpses had been ripped open and torn to pieces.

Others were still whole and unmoving in their cocoons.

Ken wondered what he would find when he finally located his son. Derek had said his mother wasn't moving.

So would Maggie be dead? What about Hope? What about the baby?

"Kiddo?" he said. Soft footsteps behind him, the sounds of shoes treading lightly on carpet sheathed by an alien secretion.

"In here," said the voice.

Ken found the office.

He saw his son.

15

It was the fifth office. Not really an office, in fact – more of a conference room. A large table sat in the middle, the kind of thing around which high-powered attorneys haggled over even higher-powered deals, or glared at one another while deposing white-collar criminals. To one side of it, a long coffee table ran along the wall. Beyond that, a couch sat along a back wall, underneath a square that could be a flat screen TV or framed art. Impossible to tell, because everything was covered in the same sticky gobs of black and gray threads.

The monstrous excretions made everything look dirty and foul. Even the light: they covered the windows on the far wall in thick drapery-like sheets, shrouding the room in a depressed twilight that weighed on the eyes and on the mind.

Derek was on the conference table.

At first Ken was sure that his son was hurt. Nearly every inch of his skin was covered in webbing, but his face was still open to the air. Still uncovered. His eyes glistened with barely-contained terror.

"Mommy," said the boy. "Save Mommy, save Hope, save Liz!" He started crying, tears that he had clearly been containing – perhaps for hours – spilling out over his cheeks.

The depth of the boy's pain nearly brought Ken up short. So did the realization that Derek probably wasn't hurt at all. That the pain Ken had heard in his son's voice wasn't his own, but merely the pain he felt for his loved ones. Derek had always been that way. Had always been more apt to cry for others than for himself.

One time Derek accidentally knocked Hope into a tree while the two were riding their bikes. Hope cried. Derek *screamed*, terrified he had hurt her. And even when she stopped crying, he went into the house and couldn't be coaxed back onto his bike for days.

"They won't move," he whimpered now. "They won't move, they won't move!"

Ken looked at his son. Followed Derek's gaze.

Ken's breath caught in his throat. He saw Maggie's face, her eyes closed. Her form pinned against what looked like a filing cabinet, anchored there by millions upon millions of silken strands. Liz's face seemed to sprout from Maggie's chest, like she was giving birth to the two-year-old in a particularly gruesome way. But it was just an illusion, the little girl glued directly to her mother's chest by the same webbing that covered everything else.

Hope was next to them. Another caterpillar. Her beautiful, dark hair stark against her too-pale skin. Hope had always been tan. She had inherited her coloring from Ken's dad. But now she looked like a ghost of herself. A specter.

Was she dead?

"Daddy," whimpered Derek. "Daddy, wake them up."

Ken looked at the others. Everyone else had crammed into the doorway of the office, as though leery to join him in this strange place. As though peering into a mass grave.

He locked eyes with Christopher, the only member of their party who still had use of both hands. "Can you get this crap off my son?" he said.

Christopher nodded. He stepped into the office, and Aaron and Dorcas stepped in with him as though afraid to be too far away from the rest of the group.

Ken thought he saw movement outside the office. But he didn't have time to stop and digest that fact.

He turned to the still-unmoving forms of Maggie, Hope, and little Liz.

He reached out for them.

A sound stopped him. Stopped all of them.

"What about *us*?"

The voice was nasally. Old. The voice of someone who was not only accustomed to complaining, but who enjoyed it. Perhaps *reveled* in it. Ken turned quickly. On the other side of the table, laying under the windows, he saw two more cocoons. Adult-sized, a man and an old woman. The woman – the clear owner of the voice – was staring at him angrily, as though all this was Ken's fault.

"You going to help *us*?" she demanded. "My son and me've been laying here for hours. Just laying here, mind you. Not saying anything, not making any trouble. Just laying here. But I guess we're not good enough to help."

The man beside her – her son, Ken supposed – remained silent. But he didn't look patient. He looked petulant. Taciturn.

Dorcas moved into the room. She almost slipped on the webbing that coated the floor, but caught herself on the table, moving around toward the pair under the window. "We'll help you," she told them.

"About time," said the old woman.

There was a tearing sound. The shearing noise of threads being torn apart. Ken saw Christopher pulling the first strands away from Derek. Freeing his son. His boy.

And that was when everything exploded.

16

The walls, the ceilings. It had all seemed so thick with the spun fibrils. So coarsely coated with the threads.

Now Ken saw through the open door of the conference room that there was more hiding beyond the sticky masses than just wood and tile and plaster. Much more.

Zombies. As though the sound of his son being torn loose had awoken them from a slumber, they erupted from dozens of hiding spots in the web-coated walls and ceilings, ripping free of the sacs where they had rested for some unknown purpose.

In an instant the deserted office suite was filled with dozens of the things. They growled, the same as the zombies that Ken and the others had been dealing with until now. The sound punched out, slammed at Ken's mind and soul. Crying at him to give up. To join them.

Derek screamed. The scream was as bad as anything Ken had yet experienced.

One or two of the things coming at them had bristly growths on their faces. Tumorous excrescences, with thick hairs, about the size of quarters. Dark and easily visible even at a distance.

What the hell are those?

Not important, Ken. Move!

Then his view was cut off as Aaron slammed the conference door shut. There was a lock and a deadbolt on this side. The cowboy engaged both. "Get your family moving," he said. Calm. Always calm. But his face was pinched, and he stood by the door, ready for the things to get through.

And they *would* get through.

Ken didn't have to be told twice. Christopher turned back to tearing the strands from around little Derek's form. Dorcas started shredding the moist threads that bound the old woman and her son beyond the conference table.

Ken knelt down and felt Maggie's throat. He had to dig under some of the webbing to get to the hollow where her pulse could be found. The strands were sticky and moist. Sickening.

Her heart was beating. He checked Hope. Liz.

Both alive.

"Maggie," he said. Then shouted. "Maggie!" She didn't move.

Something pushed his leg. It was Derek. The boy was lurching against him. He seemed to be moving oddly. Uncoordinated. Ken didn't know if that was because he'd been motionless for hours, or because the webbing had a narcotic or numbing effect. Either way, it took Derek several attempts to grab his mother's face.

"Mommy," he shouted. "Mommy, wake up!"

"Move," said Dorcas. She yanked the kid out of the way, and Ken saw that she had found a bottle of water somewhere. He looked over and saw that Christopher had taken over her position, pulling the last webbing away from the old lady and her son. They were a dour pair, both dressed in shredded business attire, both gray of hair and countenance. Neither helped him pull the webbing away, they just waited for the young man to do the work, like he was a servant.

The conference room door started pounding, almost *bouncing* against its frame. It was a solid door, with a steel frame and perhaps even a steel core if the law firm was particularly security-minded. But how long would it last?

Dorcas unscrewed the water bottle she had found, wincing as she used her bad hand for the movement, then tossed some against Maggie's face.

Maggie's eyes fluttered. Dorcas repeated the movement, this time drenching Hope and the baby as well.

Hope sniffled. Started making noises. Maggie coughed.

"Maggie?" said Ken.

The door started crackling. The growling on the other side of it got louder.

Christopher moved next to Ken and started tearing the three girls loose from their bindings.

Maggie opened her eyes fully. They moved in circles, unfocused. Unseeing. He wondered what had been done to her. Wondered if she would wake up as his wife.

A moment later she saw him. Smiled.

"Ken?"

He smiled back. "She's awake," he said to no one in particular. Then spun as though to announce it to the world. "She's awake!"

No one seemed to share his excitement. He couldn't blame them. The door was shaking in its frame. Cracking and shimmying. Then he heard one of the zombies outside the door cough. There was a wet *blat*, muffled but audible even through the thick office door.

The door started to smoke. A hole appeared in the wood, eaten through by the acid the things were now producing. An eye could be seen, enraged and insane.

It seemed to focus on Ken.

The things shrieked.

More coughs.

More smoke.

They were coming in.

17

"Help me!" Ken started yanking more of the thick, gooey threads from his wife and children. Hope woke up as he did so. More when Dorcas emptied the rest of the water bottle on the six-year-old's head.

Little Liz did not wake up. Her head lolled forward, limp and boneless-seeming. Her blonde curls plastered against her neck and her sheet-white forehead.

She was alive, Ken *knew* she was alive. Because she had to be alive. He couldn't have done so much, suffered so much, to find his family less than whole.

What would he do without his baby?

She's alive, Ken.

But she's not waking up.

"What's going on?" Maggie's voice was slurred. Drifting on tides of whatever drug had been administered to her and the other girls. Ken slapped her face. Not hard, but not particularly lightly, either. It probably hurt him worse than it did her, but they didn't have time for her to wake up gracefully.

The door was rattling harder. Smoke filtered into the room, prickling Ken's nostrils. It smelled like vinegar and gunpowder: the smell of the acid these things made.

"Daddy?" Derek looked terrified. Staring at the shaking door, at the snapping teeth that were pressing through the cracks, one of the things crushing itself against the tiny opening so hard that the sharp edges of the wood were flaying the skin away from its skull. Blood flowed.

The thing coughed, and more black acid spewed. Aaron barely managed to get out of the way, the acid landing where his feet had just been and eating a hole right through the floor.

The things outside the office starting shrieking. Not growling, not trilling. Screaming. A new sound, one that Ken had not yet heard. Anger and alarm.

Ken touched Derek briefly on the shoulder. It was all he had time for. "You'll be okay," he said.

"I'm not worried about me," said Derek. The kid was staring at his sisters and mother. Looking far too old for his age.

What are we going to do?

Hope coughed. "Mommy?" she said. Six years old, her voice was normally high and beautiful, but now it was thick and muddled. She looked around and Ken could tell she didn't know where she was or what was happening.

"Ken, what's going on?" Maggie was sitting forward, pulling away from the last bits of webbing that had bound her. Little Liz hung from her chest still, but Ken saw that it wasn't just webbing that had fastened them together: the toddler hung from a front-facing baby carrier that Maggie must have slipped on sometime after abandoning the stroller in the building lobby. Technically Liz was probably a bit too big for the sling, but Ken supposed that government safety guidelines were out the window for now. Certainly it would have let Maggie move faster and not have to worry so much about keeping hold of the two-year-old on top of the two other kids.

It was a miracle they were alive.

Chut. Another gout of acid hit the floor somewhere behind him.

"Guys, we gotta come up with something." Christopher sounded like he was about to panic.

Ken wanted to join him. Wanted to just start screaming. But he didn't. He couldn't afford to do that. He was a father, a *daddy*, and daddies didn't have the luxury of giving into panic. Not if they wanted their children to stay alive.

He helped Maggie to her feet. "I don't have time to explain," he said.

She looked over his shoulder. Saw the creature that had peeled most of the skin off its face to get in. Saw the other things behind *it*, clambering to get through the rapidly-deteriorating door. She went pale, and gasped, and he knew her well enough to see the scream in her gaze, the shriek that wanted to come out.

She held her hands in front of her. Cupping them around Liz's still-unmoving form. And she didn't scream. Mommies can't afford the luxury of panic any more than daddies can.

"What do we do?" Maggie said. She helped Hope to her feet. The little girl was listless, confused. A far cry from the bright, perpetually smiling child she had been the last time Ken saw her.

"Daddy, can I help?" said Derek.

Whump.

Ken looked over and saw that Aaron had grabbed one end of the coffee table, Dorcas the other. They battered it into the face of the zombie that was pushing itself through the door like a hideous mockery of birth. The thing screamed and coughed again. The coffee table fell in half almost instantly, the soft wood succumbing to the acid. But underneath the zombie was now writhing and shrieking as the acid it had expelled ate into its own flesh as well.

Smoke filled the room.

The things outside the office were still screaming their mad, enraged scream.

And a shudder rocked the building. It felt like an earthquake.

Only there *were* no earthquakes in Idaho.

18

"What was that?" shouted Dorcas.

"Hell if I know," said Aaron. Soft-spoken as usual, though his words seemed a bit more clipped right now. He picked up one of the pieces of the broken coffee table with his good hand. Dipped it in the fizzling pool of acid that was eating a hole in the web-coated floor nearby, then slammed it through the widening slit in the door.

The wood punched right through the chest of the half-melted zombie on the other side of the door. The thing shrieked, but other than that didn't even seem to register the attack. It kept thrashing wildly, madly, pushing ever farther through the door, ever farther into the room.

Ken looked at his son. Derek was staring at him with that look that was reserved for superheroes and daddies: that look that said, "You'll save us. I know it."

Ken tried to ignore the sinking feeling in his stomach. Tried to ignore the knowledge that they were doomed.

He ran to the only possible way out. The window. He, Aaron, Dorcas, and Christopher had climbed outside another building to escape zombies.

Of course, that was before they added six more people to their group. Several of them drugged. Three of them children.

Shut up, Ken. Just look.

He looked. Rushed to the window and pressed his face against the glass. He couldn't see anything but the reflections of the gray woman and her gray son, standing there and staring at him like they were irritated he hadn't come better equipped to handle the situation. There wasn't a good angle to see anything on the outside face of the building.

The building shuddered again. More violently this time, fairly rocking on its foundation. Maggie had to lean on the web-covered desk, Derek and Hope fell into their mother for support. Christopher and Dorcas weaved on their feet. The gray mother and son pair went down in a pile, both complaining about the weight of the other on legs and arms.

Only Aaron didn't seem to notice the impossible tremor, simply stabbing another piece of wood through the disintegrating door as though hoping to pin the reaching zombies in place.

Ken spun. Picked up a chair. He swung it as hard as he could. It went through the office window and kept going, careening through with the pealing crash of glass shearing apart. The window sailed away.

"What the hell are you doing?" shouted the gray man, still writhing under his mother on the floor. "You got glass all over me!" He was a big man, tall and broad and solidly-built, but he sounded like a spoiled child who had just been told his party was over early.

A sound came through the now-open space. Deep. Thrumming.

The building rolled again.

Ken leaned out. Looked to his right. His heart sank.

There was no way to get out. Nothing to cling to. No footholds, no handholds. Just sheer concrete and glass.

Behind him, the door to the office sounded like it was about to fall apart completely.

"We gotta do something!" shouted Dorcas.

Ken looked left. His heart caught in his throat.

He looked down. And his heart *stopped*.

19

"You're kidding."

Maggie didn't scream the words. Ken almost would have preferred it if she had. Instead, they came as a whisper when he explained what they were going to do – what they all *had* to do.

Boise had been undergoing "improvements" to its downtown area for the last few years – between five and fifty, depending on whether you asked someone who was paying attention, or one of the old-timers who just liked to bitch about things. Traffic that had once been sparse at all times of the day and night, even in the most crowded parts of the downtown area, had grown congested as it was rerouted to avoid construction areas. Scaffolding had sprouted like skeletal fungus, protecting construction workers from traffic, and vice versa.

The Wells Fargo Center they were in had been undergoing some kind of construction. A crane that was anchored somewhere in the street far below and extended beyond the top floor had been moving house-sized pieces of steel and concrete for weeks. In the first minutes of the change, the first moments when everything ended, something had blown up at the base of the crane. It tilted, then slammed into the side of the building.

Now it was still hung up against the face of the high-rise, slung at a drunken angle as though even the inanimate objects of the old world were in a state of shock about what had happened around them. The many supports and braces of the tower crawled like a ladder up the side of the building, extending past the top level.

The bottom was engulfed in smoke, a smoldering fire still barely-visible within the billowing clouds of black.

The working jib, the long arm of the crane, extended across 9th Street, hanging like a bridge over toward what was left of a ruined building. Touching, or almost touching....

"You think we can make it?" said Christopher.

"We don't have a lot of choice." Dorcas looked at the tower, and Ken knew she was wondering what he was: if the crossbars were close enough to jump to from the window. If someone with one good hand could climb up a good sixty feet, then another hundred feet across the jib, then over to the ruined remains of the One Capital Center. Assuming the jib even extended it that far.

And could they make it with children holding on? Ken knew she was thinking that, too, because her eyes kept flicking over to Derek and Hope. Not Liz: the baby was still knocked out – he hoped – in the sling on Maggie's chest. But the other kids.

"I... I can't," said Maggie. "I can't go up."

The zombie at the door had its head all the way through. Its shoulders. The door was seconds away from cracking in half.

Ken sighed. "We have to."

"Why can't we climb down?"

No one else had seen it yet. No one else had noticed.

The building shuddered. Dorcas, still looking out the window at the tower, finally looked down.

She gasped.

20

Dorcas turned away from the window. She didn't say what she had seen. And Ken was grateful for that. "I'll go first," she said.

"Like hell," said a voice. The new guy. The gray-haired man. He was a fairly big guy, maybe six-foot-two and stocky to boot, but he jumped quickly to the window, elbowing Dorcas out of the way.

"Wait for me, Buck!" said the guy's mother.

Ken thought, *Buck*? The guy seemed more like a Sherman or a Eugene than a Buck.

Buck grabbed his mother with one hand and a web-covered chair with his other, stepping up onto the chair and then from there to the sill. His eyes widened.

"What's... what's...," he stammered. He was looking down.

Buck's mother was more direct. She just screamed.

Maggie started toward the window. Ken stopped her. "You don't need to see what's there. We just need to get going." He looked at Buck. "If you're going, go. If not, get out of the way!"

Buck looked over his shoulder at Ken, terror and irritation warring on his features, then he and his mother jumped out the window. There was a thud a moment later. Clanks.

The building rumbled again. This time the tremor didn't stop. It just kept moving through the entire building, looping rolls that made it hard to stay standing.

"How are we going to take the kids?" whispered Maggie.

"I'll take the girl," said Christopher, stepping forward. "You've got the baby."

Maggie started to protest. Ken cut her off with a gesture. "He's right. I'll take Derek, he takes Hope. You take Liz. The others are working with one good hand each, so they can't do it."

"Is he...?" Maggie's voice drifted off.

It didn't matter. Ken knew what she was trying to say. "You can trust him with Hope," he said. "You can trust Christopher with her life." He turned to Derek and said, "Can you hold tight to me, champ?" Derek nodded. "Okay. We're gonna go climbing. Don't look down."

"I won't."

The door shattered. Snarls – multiple growls – rammed their way into the room.

"Go!" shouted Aaron. "Go *now!*"

21

Ken yanked Derek upward, and at the same instant Derek's arms wrapped around his neck in a death grip, so tightly he would have worried about suffocation if he hadn't already been holding his breath.

The door fell to pieces. Completely. Utterly. Only the remains of the huge conference table between the beasts and the survivors kept them alive.

Ken propelled Maggie toward the window as Christopher picked up Hope and slung the six-year-old over his shoulder. She started screaming, kicking. Not understanding what was happening, still half-dazed from the effects of whatever had been done to her.

And Ken had to ignore it. He was only one man, there just wasn't enough *him* to do more than what he was already doing. He had to trust Christopher to save his daughter.

He shoved his wife out the window. Barely a moment to let her get her grip on the sill, get balanced.

She jumped.

She screamed in mid-air. Not because of the jump – the crane tower was only a few short feet to the left of the window, an easy jump even with an unconscious toddler strapped to you. He didn't even think it was because of the heights involved. They were on the ninth floor, easily one hundred and twenty-five feet above the ground. More. But that wasn't the frightening thing.

Not frightening at all. Not compared to what was happening. Not compared to the thing that had caused the building to rumble.

Ken and Christopher went to the window next, both of them squeezing into the opening. He glanced at the young man, once the son of Idaho's governor, now just another person running a series of wind sprints against the Grim Reaper himself.

The kid had settled Hope into a death-lock under one arm. Holding her so tightly she could barely move.

"Thank you," Ken mouthed.

Christopher nodded.

Something shoved them from behind. A not-too-subtle reminder that the zombies were in the room. That Dorcas and Aaron needed to get out, too.

Something scraped behind them. There was a scream, what Ken guessed was the sound of someone shoving the remains of the conference table against two dozen surging zombies.

Ken and Christopher jumped.

They hit the crane's tower with twin thuds. Ken was holding his son with his bad hand, the one that was missing two fingers. Agony speared up through his wrist and his arm. His other arm felt only marginally better, the impact making his shoulder feel like it was on the verge of twisting out of its socket.

"Daddy, I can hold on," said Derek.

Ken looked at his son. The boy didn't wait for an answer, just spun around Ken's midsection like he was on the jungle gym at the playground. Then his hands went around

Ken's neck again. "Gotcha," said his son. He could almost hear the kid smiling. "Don't cry," shouted Derek, and Ken realized his son was trying to cheer up Hope. "The man looks nice!"

"I don't like it!" shrieked the little girl. "Who are they?"

Ken began climbing, and could tell from the vibrations in the steel that Christopher was doing the same. He looked up and saw Maggie scaling the tower right above him.

Buck and his mother were nowhere to be seen. He didn't know if they had fallen or were just far ahead. He didn't care, either.

Twin thuds. Twin tremors. Ken looked down and saw Dorcas and Aaron. Dorcas almost fell, screaming as she landed straight on her broken arm. Aaron threaded his own good arm through a crossbar and then grabbed her tank top. It stretched, almost tore.

Then Aaron grunted and yanked her back to the tower. They started to climb. Each of them one-handed.

Hope was still shrieking.

"It's okay," said Derek again.

"I don't like it!" screamed Hope.

"The man looks nice!" shouted Derek.

"Not him, *them!*"

Don't look, Derek, thought Ken. Don't look down. Don't look at what Hope is seeing.

But the boy did. Ken could tell he looked, because his son's breath suddenly sped up.

He didn't scream. Derek wasn't a screamer, not unless his loved ones were hurt. But Ken knew his son was terrified.

Because he had seen what was coming for them.

22

Ken had noted that the things, the zombies, moved as if connected. Aware of one another. They seemed to be more complete when near others of their kind, to the point that when he and Dorcas had been surrounded by hundreds, maybe thousands of the things while on top of a storage building, he had thought they almost seemed like one single organism. Like each zombie wasn't its own creature, but rather a single cell of a larger monster.

Now he saw that even more clearly. Looking down from over a hundred feet, watching as what looked like most of the population of Boise swarmed to the base of the Wells Fargo Center.

It had to be two hundred thousand of the things.

Nor did they stop at the bottom of the building. The tremors that the group had been feeling weren't what it felt like when a coordinated horde of two hundred thousand zombies mobbed the base of the building. No, it was the feeling when they were climbing *up* the building.

Ken didn't know how it was possible. But then, he didn't know how the zombies could be producing acids that ate through wood, concrete, even steel. He didn't know how they could be spinning webs. He didn't know how beating their brains out could seem to simply enrage them. How the things could exist in the first place.

It was *all* impossible.

And there they were. Scaling the side of the Wells Fargo Center, screaming and growling, the sounds of their cries grinding into Ken's mind, calling to him. It was harder and harder to keep climbing. He wanted to let go.

Only the weight of his son around his neck kept him going. Only his family kept him from giving up.

He glanced down as something hit the crane. Hundreds of the zombies were flinging themselves through the smoke that obscured the base of the massive machine. They erupted like demons from the worst parts of hell. Smoke clung to them like a garment, and some of the creatures were actually on fire.

They didn't seem to notice or care.

More of the things clambered up the side of the building. Snarling, spitting, growling. Thousands and thousands coming at Ken and the other survivors. Hundreds more coming up the crane's tower, leaping from bar to bar, from strut to strut.

He wondered if it was possible for too many people to be on a building; what would happen if too much weight fell against the already-stressed crane.

The things were fast. Faster than the survivors. Much faster.

There was a ripping sound. The crane had been hung up on the side of the Wells Fargo Center, stuck at an angle and clearly at least partially separated from whatever tethers had once kept it upright and stable.

Now it started to slip across the face of the building.

It started to fall.

23

The noise that came from the combination of metal scraping across concrete and the metal itself twisting and bending was by far the loudest thing Ken could remember hearing. Louder even than the explosions that had gone off nearby and – in some cases – right on top of him. It was loud enough that it even drowned out the sound of the throngs of zombies that were yanking themselves bodily up the crane and the sides of the high-rise toward him and the others.

The crane tipped. Vibrating as it shredded along the side of the building. And Ken couldn't think about holding onto Derek, couldn't think about Hope or Liz or Maggie. All he could think about was clamping his fingers around the nearest pieces of metal, circling his legs around the closest crossbars.

Praying.

The crane tilted. Shrieked. Stuttered to a stop. Shrieked and began tilting again. Moving toward 9th Street. Ken had been almost upright a moment ago, and now he was holding on at a seventy-degree angle. Still upright, still closer to vertical than horizontal, but being like this somehow made the crane seem like an even more precarious place to be.

It jerked and stopped moving.

Ken realized that Derek was still holding on to his neck, screaming in fear, the sudden movement of the thing that constituted their entire world wrenching terror shrieks from the boy.

But the screams were music. His boy was still here. Still safe. And maybe... maybe the shift had bought them some time.

He looked down. Hoping that some of the things had fallen, that they had lost speed at the very least.

They were still close. So close.

And then something above made a sound.

"Help!" Ken's overwrought brain registered that it was Maggie, but only barely. He was running on empty – physically, emotionally, mentally. It seemed to take everything he had just to look up.

Just to crane his neck.

Just in time to see his wife fall.

24

"Maggie!"

She hung for a second, probably less. But time is one of the indicators that whoever is behind the universe is a madman. The entirety of Ken's week-long honeymoon had only seemed to last minutes. The first years of his children's lives had come and gone in an eyeblink.

But the time he had had an infected tooth in Chile and couldn't find anyone to take care of it... three days that had lasted years. The night that Hope had had a fever that hit one hundred and five degrees before doctors managed to get her temperature under control... a lifetime.

And now, watching for the half-second before his wife let go, he felt himself grow old and die five times, ten times, a thousand times.

Then the eternal second finally – mercifully – ended. Her hands let go of the crossbar that they had been holding onto.

She fell.

Not straight down. The crane was at an angle, and she didn't plummet between the massive support beams that the survivors had been using as a ladder. Instead she slid down, falling past Ken and Christopher with a scream, twisting –

(*Protecting the baby, she's falling on her back to protect the baby but now she can't grab onto anything, dear God, Mags, turn around!*)

– so she was face-up, reaching for Ken as she slid past him. He reached for her. Too slow.

Christopher tried to grab her as well. Missed. Hope screamed, "Mom*meeeeee!*" the final syllable seeming to trail after the little girl's mother as Maggie plummeted downward.

She careened past Dorcas, who was watching with an agonized look on her face, clearly wishing she could do something. But the older woman could barely hold herself onto the steel frame that had become so ephemeral beneath them, let alone grab another person.

Then....

"Oof!"

The sound of bodies hitting, of wind thumping out of lungs, was audible. Painful.

Aaron had somehow jumped down and over. Putting himself in the path of Maggie's fall. She collided with him, her legs smashing into his shoulders, then rolling over him in a strangely balletic move before continuing down.

Like Dorcas, Aaron had only one hand. He had already done the impossible, moving like that. But even he couldn't grab onto the woman and her child.

Maggie kept falling.

25

Down. Down. Maggie tumbled over Aaron's body, over him. Past him.

Ken's vision telescoped. There were still easily a hundred thousand of the zombies at the base of the Wells Fargo Center, clustered so closely together that they looked like an oil slick. But more terrifying were the tens of thousands that were scaling the sides of the building, crawling impossibly upward, somehow sticking to the sheer walls, pulling themselves toward the survivors.

And worst of all were the shrieking monsters that were crawling up the crane itself. Smoke billowing from below them, fire coming off their clothing and their very skin. It was a view of Hell worse than any biblical vision from Revelation.

Most of the things were still fairly far away. But one of them had broken away from the horde. It was a huge creature, at least six-foot-six and broad to match. Pure muscle, from what Ken could see, dressed in what had once probably been jeans and a tank top.

The thing was a terrifying mixture of light and dark. The zombie's skin was utterly white to the point of being pink. Ken suspected that the thing must have been an albino before the world ended – unless this was one more symptom of the change.

But the white, unblemished skin was only on the thing's left half. Beyond that, a line bisected the thing neatly down the middle, separating it into right and left halves.

On the right half, there was no white skin, no trace of once-humanity. All was black and crimson. Charred by the fire the zombie had willingly gone through to get at its prey. Its skin sloughed off in ragged sheets, exposing bone and muscle that were just as dark and burnt as the skin above them.

Maggie screamed. Not just terror, but pain. So did Aaron, and Ken's vision snapped back to his wife and the heroic older man.

The cowboy had down his work well. He hadn't stopped Maggie's tumbling fall, but had slowed it enough that she could reach up and grab something.

Aaron's leg.

Maggie dangled, her back to the structure of the crane's tower. Liz's head slumped forward and down, as though the toddler were curious to see what lay below them.

The black/white monster growled, a noise louder than the others' shouts. It sounded almost triumphant.

It was only perhaps fifteen feet below Maggie's dangling tennis shoes. Close to her, and coming fast.

26

Aaron was screaming. It was the first time that Ken could remember the cowboy making a sound like that. He realized the older man was holding onto the bars of the crane with his good hand *and* had somehow wrapped the mangled fingers of his right hand around a bar as well. Trying to hold onto Maggie's weight.

"I'll get her," Ken shouted. But there was no way that was going to happen.

Christopher started moving down. Grappling with the still-writhing Hope, but clearly game to try and help Maggie.

Dorcas had no chance. Her arm was too shattered for her to do anything but hang on; try to climb.

And the black/white monster was now within ten feet of Maggie.

Ken had survived all this. He had kept himself alive, had saved others.

I'll think of a way.

Zombies on the walls.

What can I do?

Zombies under us.

I've got to think of something.

My wife. My baby.

Nothing was coming.

He had nothing.

He realized that his only options were to climb down and die, or climb up and save himself and his son, but live with the fact that he had abandoned his wife and baby.

He couldn't make either choice.

But even the refusal to make a decision, he knew, was essentially a default to the latter alternative.

Maggie screamed.

The huge zombie grabbed her foot.

27

No one knew what to do. Everyone was frozen.

Everyone but one.

Derek.

The nine-year-old moved. Too fast for Ken to react, too fast for Christopher to catch.

"Mommy!" he screamed, and suddenly his weight was gone from Ken's shoulders. The boy flung himself off Ken's back, jumping from his father's flesh to the steel of the crane and then climbing down so fast he was a blur.

"Stop him!" shouted Ken.

Christopher and then Dorcas each reached for the boy in turn. He danced out of range of both, agile as a monkey.

The creature, the black/white beast, had pulled itself up to Maggie's legs. One bite was all it would take. One bite, and she would be gone in a matter of seconds.

The zombie opened its mouth.

"Not...," screamed Derek, rushing down headfirst past Aaron...

... the zombie reared back...

"... my...," the boy continued...

... the white/black abomination thrust its face toward Maggie's leg...

"... MOTHER!" Derek finished, kicking off into space.

The zombie bit down.

28

The teeth sunk into flesh.

The world seemed to fall silent.

There was only wind. The sound of smoke puffing past. And a scream.

"NO!"

Ken didn't know who screamed. If it was him, or Maggie, or someone else. It didn't matter.

All that mattered was the sight of his boy. The sight of Derek, who had always been the one to take care of his sisters, who had always seemed more aware of others' pain than of his own, putting himself between his mother and baby sister and the looming threat.

The sight of the beast biting the child's arm.

The sight of Derek, looking up at the sky. His mouth opening.

And then sound returned as Derek screamed. Not in pain, but madness. His eyes clouded over, and everything that had made him so special was suddenly... just... *gone*. Gone, and he was one of them.

Bloody sweat exploded from the boy's pores. His body convulsed with the change, and that bought them all some time. His hands and feet punched out, and his little foot caught the black/white demon under the chin. The thing growled and let go of Maggie to grab Derek... what had *been* Derek. To do so, the monster also let go of its hold on the crane.

Derek and the black/white beast fell, both of them snarling with rage, reaching for Maggie and Liz as they plummeted. They disappeared into the smoke that still billowed up from the base of the crane.

"They're gone."

Someone yanked at Ken. Christopher, he thought. But he couldn't be sure. A weight fell on his shoulders. A crying something.

The voice came again. "They're *gone*. Take care of your daughter."

"Shhh," said Ken. Not even sure why he was saying it. Part of him realized that Christopher had passed Hope to him, then had gone down to help Maggie and the others. But the greater part of him – the part of him that mattered – didn't understand why he was saying it. Why he was doing anything.

"Get *moving*, dammit!"

Again, he thought that was Christopher. And again, he couldn't be positive. Ken moved his feet mechanically, just as he kept whispering, "Shhh," mechanically, and wasn't even sure if he would have noticed if Hope stopped crying.

He couldn't hear much. Just his son's scream, "Not my MOMMY!"

Just his son's next scream, the pain of being bitten and then the rage as he became what had bitten him.

And then the words, "He's gone." Over and over in Ken's mind.

The crane listed again. Shuddering.

"Shhh," he whispered. He kept crawling as the crane continued its mad tilt. "It's okay. Everything's okay."

And he did not care that he lied.

29

The sound of the crane continuing to tilt must have been at least as loud as it had been before, but Ken's ears seemed to have been stuffed with cotton. He barely heard the noise. There wasn't enough room in his mind to hear what was going on around him and also replay the images of recent past.

The thing that brought him back to the moment was a strange prickling in his stomach. The sensation was unnerving, one that he couldn't place for a moment. Then he realized it was weightlessness, the feeling of his body hitting nearly zero-gravity as the crane dropped out from under him.

Then the massive apparatus stopped moving, arrested by some piece of the Wells Fargo Center, or by the jib hitting part of the high-rise across the street. Either way, Ken fell into the metal with bone-crushing force. Hope, still clinging to him, screamed even louder and he realized that she was relying on him. She would die if he didn't get her out of here.

He clamped an arm tightly around her. Not as a rote motion, but like it mattered. He kissed her hair, surprised for some reason at how warm the top of her head was. She felt like she had been running around outside on a summer day.

Would there ever be such a thing again? Or had winter come to stay?

"I'm here," he shouted. "Daddy's here!"

"Daddy?" She screamed the word back, divided into equal parts terror, surprise, and faith. The monsters were here, but now Daddy was here, and he would save her.

Ken hoped her belief was less misplaced than Derek's had been.

Forget about that. That's not for now. Time for that later.

What if there is no later?

He climbed. He didn't look down, didn't look back. His wife was back there. Liz was with her. Dorcas and Christopher and Aaron, too.

But right now, the world – his whole world – was in his arms, and he had to climb away from the nightmare below. He held Hope, and she was fragile and bright, and he couldn't lose her.

The crane shuddered. Hope screamed, almost barking in her fear.

"It's okay!" he shouted. But he didn't believe it. Not now. He could feel the *thrum-thrum-thrum* of feet and hands pounding up the crane. Could feel the horde pressing up the walls of the Wells Fargo Center. Could feel the very air thickening with the presence of the *things* coming ever closer.

Then he was at the end of his climb. He flipped over the edge of the tower, and onto the jib. The jib, the projecting arm of the crane that was used to move large pieces of equipment and material, extended in both directions, forward and back. The counter jib stuck into the air high overhead, giving a final defiant middle finger to the forces that were bringing it down.

The other end of the jib, the working jib, thrust downward at a steep incline. There was a catwalk-like sheet of metal that Ken thought he could walk on, but even so the angle of it scared him. One misstep and he would just go screaming forward until he either hit the end of the line or slipped off sideways, plummeting into one hundred fifty feet of empty space, to die or be caught by the zombie mob pressed into the streets below.

Hope must have seen the same thing he did. He felt her arms tighten around his neck and chest. "Daddy," she whimpered.

And now he did look back. He saw Aaron and Dorcas, clinging to each other as though signed up for the world's strangest three-legged race. Only they were running a two-handed race up a steep incline of steel bars and crosspieces. And no awards for second place.

Beyond them, Christopher was with Maggie, the young man seeming to push Ken's wife upward half by physical force, half by sheer charisma.

Ken couldn't see Liz's face. He had to trust the toddler was still attached to her mother, and still alive.

Beyond them... darkness. A thick black clot of bleeding, burning, smoking zombies. Climbing closer. Gaining.

"Hurry!" shouted Ken.

The others seemed to step faster.

Ken turned to the gangplank.

He stepped forward. One hand encircling Hope tightly, the other reaching blindly for a handhold. As soon as he found one he took another step and repeated the process.

Step by agonizing step. Moving far too slowly. Knowing that to move faster would be inevitably to fall and to die. Knowing also that the zombies would hurl themselves forward without fear of death, single-minded in their attempts to reach their prey.

Step by step.

Clanks behind him. He looked over his shoulder. Dorcas and Aaron had made it. Then Christopher and Maggie. Liz still limp in the carrier on his wife's chest.

Maggie locked eyes with him. She was crying, the tears marking white paths through soot-stained cheeks. She reached out, her fingers extended toward him.

Ken didn't know exactly what she was reaching for. The memory of their family, perhaps. The world and life they once had. His protection. Maybe even... just *him*.

Christopher said something, grinning that infectious grin of his as he urged her forward, onward.

Downward.

Ken turned back around. He kept moving.

The end of the working jib looked like it had slammed into the side of the building across 9th Street. If so, they might be able to get from one building to another via this strange bridge.

But it was impossible to really tell. The jib could go right through the building's walls. It could also end twenty feet away. Perspective was a funny thing. And when you added panic, smoke, and a few hundred thousand building-scaling zombies into the mix, it got even weirder.

Clank, cla-cla-cla-clank. The sound of the group slamming over the catwalk suspended high above concrete and a horde of monsters did nothing to help Ken's peace of mind.

Then something popped. A loud *ping* as of a steel tether letting go.

The entire crane shifted. Laterally, this time. It pitched forward. Stopped. Again.

74

A hard lurch.

Ken lost his grip.

30

Ken went down on his back. Hard. A fraction of a second later he heard matching thumps and thuds that told him the rest of the group fared no better. He had only the barest moment in which to wrap both arms around Hope's body before he began to slide down the catwalk.

The horde below them surged and screamed, the zombies climbing over one another as though aware that they were only moments from seeing their enemies plummet to their midst.

The metal of the catwalk was far from smooth. It was pocked by bolts, rippled by the forces that had sheered the crane off at its base. Still, Ken flew along it with the speed of a bobsledder. Screaming, holding to Hope.

The end coming close. Closer.

Closer.

And he could see now that the jib didn't touch the building beyond. It ended in mid-air, in dead space. He couldn't tell how far it stopped from the side of the other building.

He tried to reach for something that would stop him and Hope from flying out into the void, but they were moving too fast. The bars and braces of the crane's lattice-like supports whipped by so fast they were a blur, and the only thing that happened when Ken reached out once was that there was a light *bwang* that was swallowed up instantly in the enormity of the crane's structure, and he felt his arm go numb with the impact.

He couldn't stop them.

They flew toward the end of the jib.

And off into nothing.

31

The building that the jib leaned toward was the One Capital Center.

Or rather, what was left of it.

The building had been hit by an Air Force stealth fighter in the first minutes after the change had coursed through fifty percent of the world's population. The jet had hit the building and exploded, blowing the upper floors clean off the building, shooting them – virtually intact – into the air.

Ken hadn't seen any of that. He and his friends only surmised it when they saw pieces of the stealth fighter, and had come across the top three floors of the One Capital Center sitting across the street several blocks over from where they belonged. The building had proved to be a necessary escape route, though it had also cost Ken the two smallest fingers of his left hand to use it.

And now he was headed back to the rest of the ruined building. Not walking, but flying. Screaming through space, shot off the end of the crane's jib like some bizarre human cannonball.

He and Hope fell, forward and down, in a short flight that ended faster than Ken was expecting. They hit and rolled, Ken cupping his body around his daughter, trying hard not to crush her. He felt glass bite his arms; felt other, harder things push into his flesh as well. But he didn't see anything – his eyes were screwed shut so tightly his head ached. As though his body were convinced that if he saw what was happening, it would be the end of their momentary reprieve.

They stopped rolling.

Ken opened his eyes. He didn't want to, but he knew that to lay wherever they were with his eyes closed would amount to a particularly stupid kind of suicide.

He opened his eyes, and saw a pair of cowboy boots about to slam right into his face.

Ken jerked to the side, and the boots slid past him, followed by the rest of Aaron. Dorcas, too, the older woman clinging to the cowboy.

Ken got to his knees. He saw that he and the others had been catapulted into the remains of one of the floors of the One Capital Center. Everything was rubble, the effects of a building that had been hit by a plane carrying some serious weaponry. No way of telling what floor they were on, but it wasn't the first one.

"Help!"

Ken's hand shot out. He grabbed the newest person sliding across the detritus-coated surface of this place. He felt fingers curl around his palm, and realized that it was Maggie. She had slid into range, still on her back, little Liz lolling on her chest.

He caught his wife.

Hauled her to her feet.

And held her. The horde was coming, but for a moment he didn't care. He needed to hold onto Maggie. To remind himself she was here, she was really here. Without thought, another hand went around Hope, pulling her to him. The family.

"Derek," she sobbed.

"I know," he said.

Then they were silent. Not long. Just a second. Just long enough to *be*. Just long enough for the world to take note that it hadn't won. Not completely. The family – part of it, at least – was still alive. Bruised, fragmented, but still holding on.

"Guys…," said Christopher. Ken looked over. The kid had appeared as though by magic. He was probably the most sure-footed of the group, so no surprise that he would have made the leap across the gap with the least trouble.

Ken sighed internally. Ready for Christopher to point to the crane, to where the hordes would be screaming across.

But he didn't. He was looking the other way.

There was something behind Ken.

Something *already there with them*.

32

Fear surfed electric waves up and down Ken's back. The hordes had come in behind them. It must be that. They were surrounded.

Then he heard Aaron curse. Not a fearful curse, more a resigned one. The sound of a soldier dealing with tragedy, not terror.

"Cover the girl's eyes," said Aaron. His voice a reverent whisper.

Ken did, putting his hand across Hope's eyes even as he turned.

It was Buck. Sobbing, kneeling on the floor before a pile of wreckage whose once-purpose Ken could not even begin to guess at. No doubt once an integral part of this room, this building, now it was just a tangled collision of steel and trash and concrete; wood and plaster and melted bits of plastic.

And flesh.

The gray man knelt before his mother. The old lady's mouth was working, opening and closing and opening and closing as though she had been caught in the grips of the world's worst indecision.

She looked at the others. Only her eyes moved. Her head did not shift. It couldn't. A thin shaft of metal – perhaps a piece of a cabinet, maybe the support bar of a desk organizer – jutted out of her cheekbone, disappearing into her skull and pinning her to the junk pile that had somehow melded itself to her.

Her mouth opened again. This time blood drooled out. The old woman's body was broken. Bent in too many ways to count, probably shattered a hundred different ways inside.

"Help... me...," she whispered.

Growling erupted behind them.

Ken looked back. The things that had been following them up the crane were now running down the jib. They *coated* it, swarming over the gangplank, climbing along the outside supports, even hanging like rabid monkeys from underneath it. He couldn't even see the metal.

"Come on," he said, and started to move. One hand holding Maggie's hand, the other still shielding Hope's face.

Buck spoke, the man's voice much different now than it had been before. It had lost its haughtiness, its entitlement. Humility had been forced upon him. "Wait," he said. "We can't leave her."

Ken was saved from having to respond by Aaron. The cowboy was gruff, direct. And honest. "She's dead already. And we have to leave."

"Don't... don't... leave... me...." The woman's voice was a gurgling whisper, a brook burning away to lifelessness under a relentless sun.

Buck looked at the others. "Will they let her die?" he asked.

Ken didn't know. And he could tell that the others didn't know, either.

Buck dissolved into tears. He buried his face in his mother's chest, and looked for all the world like a child after a hard day at school.

Aaron slung Dorcas' arm around his shoulders, and they moved toward the other end of the area, where there was a hole that might once have been an exit. Ken couldn't tell if the cowboy was supporting Dorcas, or if she was supporting him. He supposed they probably didn't know, either.

"I can't let them turn her!" shouted Buck.

Christopher followed after Dorcas and Aaron.

"I can't!" Buck was shrieking now. His voice a piercing, whining whistle.

Ken took Maggie and Hope and limped after the others.

The growl of the horde close behind. The sobs of the grown man-child even closer.

33

Ken followed the others into the hole. There was nowhere else to go: all else was collapsed wreckage, destruction, and behind them an empty area that was sure to be swarming with zombies soon. So he walked into darkness, still hearing the sounds of Buck sobbing behind.

He almost ran into Aaron. The older man was moving back toward the area they had just left, Dorcas pulling on his arm.

"Don't," she said.

"Ain't right to leave her like that," he said.

"There's no time," she said, her voice caught halfway between a whisper and a cry.

"Don't matter."

Aaron moved past Ken and his family.

Ken looked at Dorcas. "Is he…?"

She nodded.

A moment later, there was a muffled snap. A sigh.

And then Aaron came back, this time with Buck under his arm. The balding man's eyes were teary, but he seemed aware. As they came out of the light, he moved Aaron's arm away.

"Thank you," said Buck. "I couldn't. I just… I couldn't."

"I couldn't if it'd been my mother, either," said Aaron.

Buck nodded.

Something cracked outside. The building shuddered.

"What was that?" said Maggie.

Aaron looked through the faux door into the area they had just left. He glanced through furtively, as though looking around a doorway where he suspected armed enemies might be hiding.

While he was looking, Maggie whispered in Ken's ear, "Did he kill that old woman?"

Ken nodded. Maggie put a hand over her mouth. Ken looked at her, trying to tell her to stay quiet. Now was not a good time to have a conversation about the ethics of mercy-killing.

It worked. Sort of. She didn't say anything, but she looked at Aaron with an expression of supreme distaste.

She doesn't know him. She's been asleep. She doesn't understand what's been happening.

But Ken wondered if that was true. He hoped it was. But he couldn't deny that Maggie also seemed to be looking at *him* strangely. As though he was not only a part to the mercy-killing, but a party to murder.

She's reeling. From all this.

She's going to blame you.

He was saved from that line of thinking by Aaron as the cowboy drew back into the room. "Crane just tipped."

"It fell over?" Christopher said. He was smiling hopefully.

Aaron shook his head and gave a strange half-shrug. "Not all the way. Looks like it tipped and hit the building a floor or two down."

Silence.

"What does that mean?" said Maggie.

"It means they're below us," said Ken. "And we've got to figure out a way past them."

There was a muted shudder. A soft sound that might have been a roar, separated by concrete and glass and steel.

"And we've got to do it fast," said Dorcas.

34

Everyone looked around. Even Hope, clinging once again to Ken's neck, seemed to be peering around the darkened area in which they had found themselves. Taking stock as quickly as possible, knowing it was only a matter of minutes – perhaps less – before the things were upon them again.

It looked like they were in what had once been a hallway. Hard to tell, because the explosion the jet had brought with it had wrought near-absolute destruction. But there were detached doors and what looked like wall panels in the jagged space.

There was a click, and a light bloomed in the darkness. Buck was holding a small LED penlight, the kind that attached to a key ring. He swung it in a circle, eyeing the dispersed group.

"Where do you want me?" he said.

"Here," said Aaron. The cowboy gestured for Buck to join him at the opposite end of the destroyed passageway.

Buck seemed to stiffen. Whether he viewed what Aaron had done as a mercy or not, Ken couldn't see him wanting to be with the other man right now. But he moved to the cowboy without complaining. Aaron pointed, and Buck aimed the flashlight where Aaron indicated.

"Come on," said Ken. He grabbed Maggie and they moved with Hope and Liz toward whatever Aaron was inspecting.

Christopher got there a moment before they did. "What is it?" said the young man.

Aaron was pulling back some trash, a few felled panels and bits of concrete. Grunting as he did it one-handed. Revealing a metal sheet beneath.

"Can't get through that," said Dorcas. Watching from eyes veiled by pain and exhaustion.

"Bet we can," said Aaron. He pushed down another piece of trash. Revealing another metal piece. And now Ken realized it wasn't just a random sheet of steel tossed out of place by the explosion. It was a door. Two doors.

"An elevator," said Buck. He looked at the destruction around them. "I don't think it's going to be running."

"Me either," said Aaron. He put his good hand into the crack between the doors. "Help me with this."

Christopher moved up, and the two of them levered the doors apart.

As the doors opened, the growling that had only been a suspicion strengthened into a reality. The things were here. Close, and getting closer.

As always, the sound carried with it an undercurrent of hopelessness, a call to just give up, to lay down and let fate run its course. Like the fight had already been lost, and Ken and his friends were just struggling against the inevitable.

Ken held Hope close to him. Listened to her heartbeat. Smelled the acrid scent of her little girl's sweat, and tried to convince himself that *this* was what was real. That *this* was what was worth believing in, and fighting for. Family. Community.

Life.

"What's the plan?" said Christopher, peering into the darkness beyond the elevator doors.

Aaron smiled oddly. And then, in an imitation of an old-fashioned elevator operator, he said, "Going down."

35

Ken did what everyone else did when Aaron said that: he let his mouth hang open for half a second, then he pushed forward to see what was beyond the elevator doors.

He wasn't sure whether he was more surprised at the fact that Aaron was saying they were going to go down, or the idea that the cowboy had done it in a joking fashion. Aaron had never made a joke before. Maybe the ongoing apocalypse was convincing the older man to let his hair down. Maybe he was just determined to go down smiling. Maybe Christopher was a bad influence on him.

But no matter his reasons, the idea of "going down" *had* to be a joke.

Because there was nothing beyond the doors. At least, nothing that looked like it could be used to go down. Just empty space and some mangled machinery.

"Are you nuts?" said Dorcas.

Buck nodded, looking a bit irritated for a second, like Dorcas had stolen his line in the play.

Aaron shook his head. The joking now gone from his expression. "Safest way down. We already know they go up stairs faster than we do, and now they're climbing up the walls, for goodness' sake." He gestured at the darkness beyond the elevator doors. "Nothing to climb in there."

"Uh...." Christopher raised a finger as though he was in a classroom, waiting to be called on by the teacher. "Yeah, so how do *we* get down then?"

Aaron took Buck's light. He pointed it at the machinery. It looked like a large spool, hung up on the side of the elevator shaft, partially embedded in the concrete wall. Several thick metal cords trailed off it, disappearing into the darkness like the limp limbs of a giant daddy longlegs that had been smashed by an even larger boot.

"That there," said Aaron, pointing at the spool, "is called the greave. Those lines sticking out of it are the elevator cables."

"And?" said Christopher.

"And by federal law, each one of those cables is required to be strong enough to hold up the entire elevator at full capacity."

"So?" said Buck. A bit of the haughtiness back in his voice.

"So that's more than enough to hold each of us," said Aaron.

Silence.

"How do we hold on?" said Dorcas. She motioned at her broken arm. "We got broken arms, banged-up hands. Kids."

Aaron grinned tightly. "I happen to know a few tricks."

"Tricks?" said Dorcas. "For going down a dark elevator shaft using elevator cables with one arm, holding onto kids?"

"Something along those lines."

More silence. Broken only by the groans filtering up from below. Finally Christopher said what Ken supposed they were all thinking.

"Who *are* you, man?"

36

Aaron tipped an imaginary hat. "Aaron. Pleased to meetcha."

"You know that's not what I meant," said Christopher. "What do you *do*?"

"Honest answer?"

"Yes."

Aaron sighed. "Most recently... and this is God's truth... I was a rodeo clown."

No one spoke for the space of perhaps ten seconds. Finally Buck said, "You. Are. Shitting me."

"Language!" Maggie snapped the word, holding her hands over Hope's ears. Ken almost laughed. It was absurd. They were fighting over whether or not to climb into a vertical coffin, climbing down – in some cases one-handed – into darkness in order to avoid zombie hordes that to all appearances had taken over the world. And Maggie was worried about Hope's exposure to profanity.

But then, wasn't that the point? What was the reason for living, if not to show our children at the very least the *possibility* of a better world? If life became nothing more than survival, then humanity was already dead. Homo sapiens might go on as a biological classification, but it was only in the expression of our better selves that we could find something beyond *existence*. That we could find meaning.

He squeezed Maggie's arm.

"No, sir," said Aaron. "I was a rodeo clown. Last few years. Good job."

"That's not where you learned to do this," said Dorcas. Her voice was quiet. Intense.

Aaron looked at her, and even in the shaky illumination of the small flashlight, Ken could see the cowboy's face change. The older man wouldn't lie to Dorcas. But nor would he tell her everything.

"No," said Aaron. "But that's a story for another day." He looked back into the shaft. "For now, just trust me." He swung back to stare at them as the growling grew louder. "Please. We don't have a lot of time."

Buck shook his head.

"You're all insane." He stepped back the way they had come. Toward the waiting corpse of his mother.

Ken thought he might be right. This... how could they do it?

Buck looked at them. "Well?" he said. "Anyone coming?"

And at that moment the world fell in on him.

37

Like everyone else, Ken had visions of 9/11 burnt into his mind from news images, repeat airings of first-person footage, countless ratings-grabbing "special reports" over the years. He remembered seeing people emerge from clouds of dust and ash, covered so completely in the stuff they looked like ghosts. And that was what Buck looked like when he stumbled out of the vast white cloud a moment later.

"What...?" he coughed. "What happened?" He almost collapsed. Christopher caught him, pounding the man's back as he hacked and spit to clear his throat.

Aaron was swinging his flashlight at the huge cloud that had enveloped Buck. The powder and dust refracted the light weirdly, seeming almost to eat it. "Collapse," said Aaron.

He turned the light back on Buck. "He all right?"

Christopher nodded. "I think so." He looked at Aaron. "Any way out through there?"

"Not anymore."

"You have a helluva way of convincing people to do things your way," said Christopher. He was grinning as he said it, but the grin looked a bit fractured to Ken.

Aaron nodded as though taking the words at face value. He returned to the elevator doors and disappeared into the narrow crack in the darkness.

Ken could just see him, shuffling around a narrow ledge that rimmed the edge of the shaft. He went to the greave and leaned down, inspecting the cables that trailed off it, pulling on each with his good left hand. Then he nodded to Christopher and the young man joined him out on the ledge.

"Rodeo clown my – uh, butt," said Buck. Then dissolved into another round of gasping coughs.

Ken didn't particularly like the bald older man, but he agreed. Whatever Aaron's story was, there was more to it than dressing up in silly paint and hiding in barrels to keep angry bulls from killing thrown riders.

Christopher laughed inside the shaft. Not a happy laugh. The kind of laugh when you've just heard something deeply disturbing. Along the lines of "You've got terminal cancer," or "You should think about getting your affairs in order."

Then Aaron said, "Buck?"

Buck looked at the others. "I guess I'm the guinea pig."

Ken expected the man to resist. But he stepped through the crack between the doors. Went over to Christopher and Aaron. The two talked to him for a moment, then Christopher lowered him into empty space. Buck disappeared from Ken's sight.

Ken expected to hear a scream. Long, fading. Then nothing.

Instead, he only heard the continuing sound of the things coming closer. He couldn't tell where they were: the open shaft bounced their growls and groans around and made it impossible to pinpoint a location.

Maggie grabbed his arm.

"Dorcas?"

The older woman shook her head. "Take the kids first," she said.

"Dorcas...." Aaron's voice carried a warning tone. Not of threat, but the sound Ken associated with a long-married man warning his wife he didn't want to get into an old argument again.

Dorcas' voice came back with the same tone. "I'm not going until they do."

Aaron sighed. "Fine."

"Who do you want?" said Ken.

"Dealer's choice."

Ken kissed Maggie, and pushed her through the doors.

38

Maggie disappeared, and Ken felt like he was losing himself again. He heard her voice, saw pie-slices of her face through the crack in the doors. She didn't sound happy, and she gave a little cry when Christopher grabbed her and helped her drop down.

Then she was gone from view.

"Where is Mommy going?" said Hope.

"She's going down where it's safe," said Ken. He hoped he wasn't lying.

"Is Lizzy going to be okay?"

"Sure she is," he said. He tightened his grip on his daughter. Sometimes he worried that he might hold her too tight, sometimes he feared he would hug her so close that he would crack her ribs – wouldn't *that* be something fun to explain at the emergency room?

But there were no more emergency rooms.

No more hospitals.

He didn't know if there'd even be a tomorrow.

So he held her as tightly as he could. Held her until she groaned.

"Ken," whispered Christopher. "Your turn."

He loosened his grip on Hope, then made sure her arms were securely around his neck. After a moment, he took the belt off his pants. He slung it around his chest, and it just went around her narrow torso as well. He cinched it through the last hole on the belt. Not much as far as safety harnesses went, but it was better than nothing.

"Hold on, okay," he whispered.

She nodded. "I'm scared."

"Me too. But if you hold on tight, maybe I'll be less scared, okay?"

She looked at him. Serious eyes that shone in the darkness. She nodded. "I'll hold you." Her arms tightened.

Ken thought of Derek. His children were good. Genuinely *good* people.

Please, God, let me save her. Let me save Liz. Let me save what's left of my family.

He stepped through the elevator doors. Onto a ledge, six inches wide and nothing below.

Please, God.

39

He only stepped in a few inches before Christopher grabbed him. The young man seemed unaware of the fact that he was dangling only inches away from a dark nothing that extended probably over a hundred feet below them. Ken remembered the way they had met, only maybe an hour – and what seemed like a hundred years – before. Christopher had saved them all from a small horde, blowing up a floor of a building, and showing them how to scale the outside of it to escape. He seemed equally at ease hanging onto a vertical surface as he did on terra firma.

"Where'd you learn to do this?" Ken asked.

Christopher laughed. "Parents kept shipping me off to taller and taller boarding schools." His smile widened. "New York was the highest."

"Come on," said Aaron. "No time for jabbering."

"Shouldn't there be a ladder?" said Ken.

Christopher pointed. There *was* a ladder. It ended about ten feet above their heads, sheared off mid-rung. Above that was a pile of rubble that didn't look very stable. Probably the remains of whatever motor room had housed the elevator equipment.

"Come on," said Christopher. He helped maneuver Ken into position, then he and Aaron dropped Ken below the greave.

Beneath the spool that held the elevator cables, things got dark in a hurry. Dark, and torn up. What Ken had assumed was a normal elevator shaft proved to be marred by tears and gaps, the cylinder obviously crooked even in the small area that he could see before darkness claimed the tunnel.

Ken felt around with his feet. The side of the shaft was crumbling nearby, and he was able to stand on some partially-pulverized concrete that formed a foothold. He didn't know how stable it was, but it was all he had.

Better than nothing.

A ghostly wail came from the darkness. The zombies in the building, searching for them.

"Now what you're going to do is rappel down," said Aaron. The cowboy was leaning down, whispering only a few inches away from Ken's face.

"I don't have any gear," said Ken.

"You ever rappelled before?" asked Aaron.

"No."

"Then you wouldn't know what to do with the gear anyway. So we're good either way."

The cowboy grabbed one of the cords and pulled it over to Ken. It didn't have much give, and when the cowboy pulled it over Ken's neck the steel cords bit into his skin.

"Ow!" Ken said.

Below him, the groans intensified. And now they sounded like they were even with him, too. Were they on the same floor?

"It's better tight. It'll tear your neck up, but better that than falling, right?" said Aaron. Ken nodded. "Now step over the cord. No," said the cowboy as Ken clumsily complied, "with the other leg." Ken adjusted. The groaning of the things was getting louder.

"They're coming," he said.

"Then move faster." Aaron instructed him on how to wrap himself up in the cord until he was cinched in a tight curl of the steel cable. There was almost no play in it, and it bit painfully against his crotch and his neck.

"Now," said Aaron. "Listen close. Step back. The cable'll hold you. Hold on with your right hand – your good hand – onto the cable that's between your legs. That'll keep you from going down too fast. You can hold your girl with your left arm."

"Okay."

"Just remember – the heights are nothing to worry about. Falling never hurt anyone. Hitting the bottom is the problem. So don't let go."

Ken waited for more. Silence. "That's it?"

"That's it."

Aaron looked over. Then back at Ken. The cowboy's face was pinched and nervous. "I'd appreciate it if you got a move on, son."

Ken nodded. "Hold on, Hope."

Hope's arms tightened around his neck.

He suddenly remembered countless cartoons from his childhood, hearing animated animals say, "Look out for that first step, it's a *doooozie!*"

He stepped back.

40

He held on tight. Tight to Hope. Tighter to the wrapped steel cables in his right hand. The fibers bit into his flesh, and he could feel the skin tearing away from his neck as he let himself fall down through the air.

Down through the darkness.

He wondered how far he should go. And answered the question as soon as he asked it of himself.

You go as far as you can, Ken. You go until you can't go anymore.

He dropped into nothing. Looked up and saw he had already fallen farther than he thought. The light where Aaron and Christopher had been was nothing but a point above him. A star in the darkest night he had ever experienced.

There was nothing else. Nothing but black and the weight of his daughter against his chest and neck.

And the groans. The growls.

The zombies sounded like they were everywhere. They sounded like they were above, below.

They sounded like they were *in* the shaft.

"Daddy," said Hope. Her voice was low. A whisper. As though she sensed danger's propinquity, and even her child-mind knew that silence was critical.

"Shhh," he said. Gentle. He didn't want to scare her worse than she must already be. Worse than *he* was, for that matter.

Still dropping, still letting steel threads slide through his clenched hand. The cable was covered in some kind of thick grease, but even that wasn't keeping friction from rubbing his skin raw. He felt like his hand was bleeding.

How far down?

As far as you can get.

He wanted to shout. To see if Maggie was near. But what if he was heard by... other things? What if his shouts drew danger rather than comfort?

He looked up. The light that had been a star was now just a hint, a dream of a memory. Then a black shape came between him and the memory and all light was gone.

He figured the dark thing must be Dorcas, lowering herself one-handed. Christopher and Aaron would be following her.

All the way down.

As far as we can get.

As far as we can go.

But he didn't go any farther. He stopped.

Because he heard another sound. Another growl. And this time it wasn't bouncing up from some unknown place below them. It wasn't reverberating off broken walls, thrown to his ears by the acoustics of disaster.

No, it was *here*.

A moment later the sound came again. And with it the smell, the warm, rotten smell of one of the things.

Inside the shaft.

41

Ken couldn't tell if the thing was on a ledge like the one that had circled the shaft behind the elevator doors above, or if it had found some piece of ladder to climb, or if it was just scaling the bare walls of the concrete tube the way the zombies had climbed the walls of the buildings outside.

Nor was there any indication how it had come to be in the elevator shaft in the first place. Maybe it was some hapless maintenance man, caught in here when the change came, converted to a mindless monster and stuck since that first instant. Then Ken realized if that was the case the others who had come this way already would have made some kind of noise of warning.

No, the zombie was a new arrival. Had to be.

The things were like cockroaches, sliding into any available crack or crevice, squeezing in to search for food.

Ken held his breath. He continued letting the cord reel through his hand, praying that Hope would remain silent.

He realized the area was starting to brighten. What had been a pitch black mystery had turned into a thick gray fog.

He looked up.

The star had returned to the sky.

The light was coming down.

Ken looked over.

And saw the zombie clinging to the wall of the shaft directly across from him.

42

The thing was facing away from him, hanging to the wall. Ken couldn't tell what it was clinging to: in the brightening light he could see that parts of the shaft were wrecked, huge pieces of concrete barely hanging to their moorings. Other areas looked smooth and unmarred.

The part of the shaft where the thing was climbing looked relatively whole, and Ken couldn't tell if it was holding to something as a man would, or if it was somehow adhering to the smooth surface of the shaft.

He could see the thing's head was tilted back, though, and it was easy enough to observe that it was tracking the light above them both.

Hope inhaled. She was going to scream. When she did, it was over. The thing would notice them. Would come for them. Would leap to them and knock them into the void, or would simply pull them to pieces right there on the cable.

Or it would bite them. Would change them.

A scuttling noise aborted the little girl's scream mid-breath. Ken looked over and saw another zombie pull itself through a crack in the side of the shaft. The crack was too small for something its size, too small by far. The zombie didn't care. It yanked itself through the crevasse, seeming to shed what remained of its clothing and the skin below it like a snake, and when it came into the shaft it was bleeding along its entire length and breadth. Impossible to tell if it was even a man or woman. Just a growling, chittering length of pulpy blood. A *thing* that stuck impossibly to the slick interior of the shaft.

Twenty feet away from Ken and his daughter. Empty air the only thing separating them.

It hadn't seen them yet.

Yet.

The two things scuttled along the wall of the shaft. Drawn to the light that was still dropping closer, closer. They climbed upward, and as they did Ken realized he could hear a subtle popping noise every time they moved their hands. It sounded like the noise you might hear pulling your foot out of a wet bog. A suction seal breaking.

They were moving toward Dorcas. He could see her now, dropping toward them. He didn't know if she was aware of them. He doubted it.

He didn't know what to do, either. Did he call to her? If he did, he would draw their attention. And die.

What would that gain the group?

He pulled Hope tighter. So tight he thought he heard her bones creak.

The two zombies, ever clearer as the star of brightness dropped closer and closer, climbed. Chittered. Growled.

Dorcas stopped her descent.

She must have seen them.

One of the zombies shrieked. That trilling call that Ken thought was meant to summon others.

Sure enough, a moment later another one of the things began pushing itself through that same crack. Peeling off its outer layers of clothing and skin on the jagged edges of the concrete rift as it yanked its way into the shaft.

And then another.

Another.

Another.

He heard something skitter behind him. Trilling.

He turned his head.

There were more of the things behind him.

They were everywhere.

43

For some reason, Ken was less frightened than he was disturbed. As though his fear had been short-circuited by some internal sense that what he was seeing was not just horrifying but *wrong*.

Humans should not be able to scale sheer, unblemished walls.

They should not be able to do what these *things* were doing.

They moved strangely in the pseudo-illumination of the small light above. Seemed to jump from place to place. One moment in one position, then Ken blinked and when he opened his eyes their configuration had changed.

There were more and more of them, too. At first just five or six, then ten, then a dozen, then twenty. Then the walls of the shaft started to disappear under a shifting blanket of torn and bleeding flesh.

Many of the things had the same tumorous growths that he had seen on the zombies that exploded out of the webbing in the attorneys' offices in the other building. Dark masses that were covered in thick hairs and looked strong as armor plating. They appeared in random blotches all over the things' bodies, and for some reason they, too, struck Ken as deeply, innately wrong. They made his skin crawl, made acid creep up into the back of his throat.

The things clambered up and down the shaft. Some of them looked at him, others stared at Dorcas. Still others seemed to be focused higher and lower – no doubt putting their sights on the others who hung helpless on the cables in the shaft.

What would happen when they were ready to strike?

Ken had his answer a moment later.

One of the zombies screamed.

And jumped.

44

The things had jumped before. When Ken, Dorcas, Aaron, and Christopher had found themselves hanging off the side of a building the things had thrown themselves off higher floors in an effort to capture them. But that had been different. That had been almost as though the things had simply shambled to the edge of the floors above, then lobbed themselves over as though reaching for their prey and having no awareness of the fact that their floor space had run out.

Now, only a few hours later, the things were leaping at the survivors in a different way. No jumbled falls, these were bursts of uncoiling energy that brought to mind pouncing jungle cats.

Not only that, but the jumps were much farther than they should have been. The monsters bunched against the shaft walls, then shoved off into space, pushing out not a foot or two, but five or six or seven or *ten* feet into the nothing of the shaft before falling with a shriek.

And even as they fell, their fingers reached, struggling to grasp what they sought. They screamed, they clawed at the air.

Above Ken, Dorcas was screaming. Below him, he could hear Maggie doing the same. He couldn't see her, but he could hear his wife calling out, screaming his name.

"I'm here, Maggie. Hold on!"

He didn't know if she heard him. Not over the sound of her own screams and those of the shrieking, falling things everywhere around him.

Hope was suddenly, oddly silent.

He looked at his daughter. She was peering at the things that filled the air around them. Her eyes almost glittered, but not with fear. He couldn't tell what the look was, but it wasn't fear.

It scared him.

"Hope?" he said.

She didn't answer.

That scared him, too.

It started to get dark.

He looked up. The star, the one bit of light in the darkness of the shaft, was disappearing. Going upward.

Soon all was black. All was starless, moonless night. A night unbroken by any illumination, filled only with the screams of hidden monsters throwing themselves at the survivors as they hung motionless in space.

45

There are many kinds of darkness.

There is silent darkness, in which you are left to wonder what may be around you, in which your mind is given free rein to improvise new nightmares and imagine new horrors. Then there is the kind of darkness where the nightmares have already been seen, and now are unseen. Where the nightmares are indisputably real, but cannot be found with any sense but that of sound and – for the most unlucky – touch.

Ken found himself in that latter darkness, holding tightly to the cable with one hand, to Hope with the other. His right leg was pinned straight down by the tension of the cable, his left leg stuck into space. He swung ever-so-slightly in the deep black nothing of the elevator shaft, and every so often he felt a breeze pass by him at the same time as he heard a zombie's scream grow loud and then soft and knew that one of the things had tried to capture him.

He was safe. They couldn't reach him.

The others were safe. The monsters couldn't reach *them*, either.

The shaft was a good thirty feet square, with the survivors hanging pretty close to dead center of the space.

Brightness again.

"Move down!"

It was Christopher's voice. That surprised Ken. He had thought it would be Aaron. But of course, the cowboy wouldn't have been able to climb *up*, not with only one good hand. So Christopher must have volunteered to come last. Must have gone back up.

But for what?

It didn't matter. He was crying out for everyone to get moving again.

Ken did, letting the cable he'd been holding onto with a death-grip start reeling out once more. He looked at Hope as the light bloomed around them again.

She still said nothing. She just watched as the zombies flung themselves into void in their rabid attempts to destroy what hung in the shaft.

Hope was mesmerized by the sight. She looked like Ken imagined a moth must look right before it threw itself headfirst into a candle, right before it erupted into a suicide of flame.

She actually started leaning away.

"No!" he shouted.

She reached for one of the things.

And it *grabbed her hand*.

46

Ken saw it unfold, but there was nothing he could do. Nothing he was going to be *able* to do. The thing was going to either rip Hope away from him, or it was going to use her as an anchor to climb up and tear both of them apart.

He honestly didn't know which would be worse.

A sound tore through the artificial night of the shaft. A tearing, rending noise. It sounded like a combination of thread unspooling on a sewing machine and meat being torn apart.

Something hit the zombie in the face. A moment later, something hit Ken in the head.

He almost lost his grip on the elevator cable. Almost forgot where he was for a moment. He'd fallen out of a two-story building today, hit his head on a freeway abutment, and concussed himself Heaven-only-knew how many times. This last was nearly the straw that broke him.

He slid a few quick feet before the pain in his neck, the agony of metal cable fibers ripping at his throat, awoke him from the half-trance he had fallen into. His good hand clenched automatically and his fall arrested. He stopped.

What had happened?

Screams. Everyone – every*thing* – was screaming.

The monsters. The survivors. Hope was shrieking, reaching downward as though for a fallen toy.

And he heard someone calling his name. "Ken! Ken, you okay?"

Dimly, he realized that it was Dorcas. That she must have seen the monster jumping at him and had slid down the cable and kicked it in the face before it could grab Hope away from him. Her other foot must have caught *him* in the head.

"Ken?"

"Yeah!" He snapped the word. Realized he was sounding ungrateful to a woman who had just saved his life and that of his child, and tried to soften his tone. Not easy when your daughter is screaming bloody murder and trying to throw herself to her death while monsters toss themselves at you from every direction. Still, he managed somehow. "Yes. I'm okay. Thanks."

Her answer was typical Dorcas. Good-natured in a to-the-point sort of way. "You can thank me by getting your butt in gear." She kicked at a falling zombie. The kick missed by a mile, but the motion seemed to make her feel better. It certainly made Ken feel better, knowing that the farm woman was as full of fight as ever and ready to protect him.

He started going down again. "Where'd Christopher go?" he called as he dropped. Trying to ignore the monsters, trying to ignore how weird it was to be having this conversation, or any conversation, under these circumstances.

Hope was still screaming. Still trying to jump away from him. He was finding it ever harder to hold onto her. What had happened to her?

"Beats me," shouted Dorcas. "How much farther down?"

Ken tried to see below them. Darkness swallowed the shaft only a few yards under his feet. "I can't tell."

"I hope it's soon."

He didn't like the tone of her voice. He looked up. Realizing at that instant that the things were no longer falling like screaming autumn leaves around them.

And he saw why Dorcas sounded worried. And why he should be worried, too.

47

Ken had observed how the things seemed to function better when they were with others like them. How when they were in ones and twos and threes they seemed somehow more awkward, less fluid. As though what had changed them had stolen not merely their ability to speak and reason, but to be alone.

As though they feared solitude.

So he had seen them grow stronger, more agile, when they were with others. He had seen the zombies cluster around one another and then crawl over and crush one another so that they could create ramps of themselves, so that they could reach higher and higher in search of their prey.

But he had never seen anything like this.

At first he wasn't even sure what it was he was seeing.

Then he understood, and wished to God he could forget.

One of the things scampered across the wall of the elevator shaft to where a piece of exposed metal had thrust through the concrete. It was jagged and sharp-looking, but the zombie didn't seem to care. It grabbed onto the metal and then just hung there.

Another zombie joined it a moment later. Running along the walls with that sickening plop-plop-plop as its fingers held, then let go, then held, then let go of the sheer surface of the shaft.

The second zombie crawled along the length of the metal spear, then onto the first beast's head and shoulders. It wrapped its arms around the other's chest, its legs around the legs of the first. Both the monstrosities were nearly bereft of skin, flayed by their entry into the shaft, their flesh torn away by the edges of the too-small rift in the concrete. It was impossible to tell if the creatures were women or men – they were only *things*, just masses of wet muscle and bone in the permanent night of the shaft.

Blood dripped off them in thick streams. It looked almost black. Ichorous. Ken couldn't tell if that was a trick of the un-light of the shaft, or if their blood, like everything else about them, was changing.

Another zombie pulled its way onto them. This one had once been a man, identifiable by the tattered remnants of a business suit and what looked like part of a tie thrown over its shoulder. The third zombie crawled onto its brother/sister things and, like the first, held tight.

Ken watched a fourth climb into the middle of the shaft and hold to the growth, then a fifth. The excrescence seemed to pulse as the zombies in the middle of the mass shifted slightly, the ones on the outside layers adjusted their grips. It was like watching a beating heart coming into being from nothing. An unholy vision of *creatio ex nihilo*.

"What are they doing?" said Dorcas. The woman's voice was low; clearly she was speaking to herself.

But with the question came an answer. Ken looked at Hope. She was still reaching out. Reaching for the dark tumescence just above them. Reaching and now she was groaning, almost....

Ken's blood ran cold.

She was almost *growling*.

And he knew what the things were doing.

"They're building a bridge," he said.   "Building a bridge to the cable. To us."

48

Ken felt... *dark.*

His wife and baby were somewhere below him. Below and unseen.

(*Dark.*)

His daughter was reaching out for the things that tried to kill them. Hands lifted up as though in praise or prayer.

(*Darker.*)

His son was gone. Bitten. Changed. Dead.

(*Darkest.*)

And then he realized with a start that the feeling wasn't merely a mood, it was a reality. That the light in the vertical tunnel that had become a sudden deathtrap was fading once more.

He looked up.

The light wasn't just fading. It was departing. Christopher was leaving them. Again.

What's he doing?

The light dimmed to almost nothing. Almost. And perhaps complete nothingness would have been better. Would have been a gift. Because as it was Ken could see just enough to make out the glistening, pulsing mass that added to itself bit by bit, that reached out inch by inch, foot by foot.

How long until one of them reaches the cable?

How long until one of them reaches us?

The things worked in near-silence, not even trilling or growling anymore. There was only the moist sloughing of flesh on flesh, of raw muscle fibers sliding across one another as they gripped and clenched with strength that was just one more impossibility in a world where the impossible had come to snuff out the once-real.

And yet, though silent, still the things moved in preternatural harmony. As though each could not only see what the others needed, but read the others' very thoughts.

Move, Ken. Move, dammit!

He knew that to stay would be to die. The things were reaching out. Grappling half-blindly in the ever-darkening stillness of the long coffin-shaft. Perhaps ten feet above where he and Hope and Dorcas hung, perhaps another seven or eight feet away from the cable. Only a few feet, only a few moments.

But he was frozen. Frozen by the sight of the monsters that were coming for him. By the things that were happening all around him. By his wounds. By his exhaustion, his hunger, his thirst.

Most of all by his daughter, his Hope, reaching for the beasts.

"Go."

Ken didn't know whether he was the one who said it, or if it was Dorcas urging him on. He didn't know if it really mattered, either. He didn't see how they could possibly outrace creatures willing to slice themselves to ribbons and able to stick to featureless walls.

Then he felt Hope's heartbeat. She was reaching for the things above them. Reaching, growling, groaning, almost *moaning* in what sounded like pleasure.

But he felt her heartbeat. He remembered holding her for the first time. Barely bigger than his hand and still trailing the lifeline to her mother. Cupping her in his palm and feeling the hummingbird-pulse of her heart as she screamed at a new and terrifying world. Feeling the softness of her skin and whispering to her that he loved her and he would be her daddy forever and he would protect her because that was his job and that was what daddies did.

He couldn't give up.

He began to lower himself again.

Looked down.

And stopped.

Another pulsing bridge of bodies had extended out over the emptiness just below them. This one even closer to the cable, the leading edge of the zombies just inches away from grabbing the thick tether.

There was nowhere for Ken and Dorcas and Hope to go.

They were trapped.

49

The things had been silent before.

Now, inches away from completing the span of flesh that would enable them to reach their prey, Ken could hear them again. Sniffling, grunting.

Growling. Always that same growl, that same wheezing noise that invited listeners to come to them. To give up. Give in.

To *die*.

He wanted to. Wanted to let go. To let it end.

Suspected it was *already* over. Even if he hadn't accepted that fact yet.

Certainly Hope seemed to want the end. She strained for the things above them, reaching up like a supplicant at the many feet of a throbbing, wheezing god made flesh.

Then she noticed the things below. She cooed. *Cooed*, like she was a baby again and had just received a shiny new toy, or had just seen her mother after a long absence. And then she was reaching not up, but *down*.

More appropriate, Ken thought, because if this *was* some strange god, then surely it was a god of darkness, of abyssal regions too black to contemplate.

The mass below them was larger than the one above. It was impossible to tell how many of the zombies were clinging to the side wall of the elevator shaft, and to each other. Ken couldn't tell where each ended, where each began. There was just a massive agglomeration of oozing arms and legs, of dripping trunks and heads partially covered by black, cancerous growths.

He couldn't see individual monsters.

But he did see the hand that reached out and grabbed the cable.

Surprisingly, the thing didn't haul itself onto the line. Didn't pull itself up to where Ken and Hope and Dorcas waited, easy spoils.

It just held.

And Ken realized that the thing didn't want to grab them itself. That wasn't its job. It wasn't its place.

Ken looked at the bridge of bodies. Saw a half-dozen things scampering across the span. And knew that *these* were the hunters. The killers. The beasts that would end his life.

Half would go up to kill him and Dorcas and Aaron and Christopher.

The others would go down and finish Maggie and Liz and Buck.

The things were not only working together now, they were strategizing.

Thinking.

The first of the things was halfway across the bridge.

It had those same plate-like growths on its face. Its cheeks were pocked with them, its forehead partially obscured. Its eyes were completely covered. Bristling growths had either enclosed them, or replaced them.

Ken expected the thing to fall blindly off the roiling mass of bodies under it. But it bounded along on hands and feet with the sure movements of a spider in its web. Roaring. Growling.

Blind, it has to be blind.

Why doesn't it fall?

The blind zombie roared.   And looked with eyeless eyes right at Ken and Hope.

The rest of the zombies in the shaft – the ones that had formed themselves into a bridge, the ones that still skittered like bloody roaches across the walls, *all* of them – shrieked as well.

50

The sound of the monsters was so loud, so deafening, so nearly *complete*, that Ken almost didn't hear... the other signals.

Almost didn't hear the low thud.

Almost didn't hear the wrenching crack.

Almost didn't hear the whistle.

But he must have heard them all. Must have, at least on some subliminal level.

He looked up.

Something was falling.

Something big.

Huge.

His first thought was that something new was happening. And new was bad. New was *always* bad, new was just this world's way of trying to kill them with more variety. Evolution was speeding up, and had focused on one task: the complete eradication of humanity.

They're growing. They're already invincible and spewing acid and they climb walls and now they're growing, *dammit!*

The thing fell from above, plummeting through the shaft like a piece of the night sky.

Invincible. Acid-puke. Stick to walls. Growing. What next?

And then a voice forced itself into his fragmented, panicked thoughts. Christopher: "Timmmberrrrr!"

Ken's fingers clenched even tighter around the cable, his arm pulled Hope so close to his chest that he wouldn't have been surprised to hear her bones creak and crack.

The whistling increased in intensity. So did the growling.

Then....

BOOM.

The falling mass hit the fleshy bridge that had built itself across the shaft above Ken and Dorcas. The zombies screeched and then seemed to shatter into ten thousand fragments. Bodies and body parts exploded in every direction. They fell past Ken.

He saw a disembodied hand, fingers still opening and closing, and he tried to convince himself that it *wasn't* reaching for him. That it *wasn't* trying to grab Hope as it passed her.

But he failed. Because he was certain that the hand was doing just that. No brain, completely disconnected. But still reaching. Still trying to kill.

Then in the next instant he saw a huge piece of what looked like rock – the mass that had plowed through the bridge above them – rocket past.

It hit the zombie with the growths covering its eyes. The thing had time for a single abortive shriek before the gray block went right through it. Then the massive chunk continued through the bridge, tearing it apart as violently as any explosive could have done.

"Look out below!" screamed Christopher, his voice still coming from the dim light far above. Ken thought wildly that this must be what it was like to talk to an angel. To hear a voice from the light of Heaven.

Sure. If God sent angels who had weird senses of humor and dropped bricks on monsters' heads.

But that was what *had* happened. Christopher must have somehow managed to climb up and loosen some of the wreckage around the sides of the shaft.

He had saved them. Again.

It occurred to Ken that he owed everyone in the company his life, many times over.

Hope was still screaming, but her shrieks were no longer the fever pitch they had been a moment ago. As though when the monstrous bridges had been torn apart, so had whatever power held sway over her.

She quieted.

But there was still screaming. Not hers, but screaming nonetheless.

It's not over.

Ken looked up.

And saw that some of the zombies had made it. Were on the cable above them.

And climbing down toward Dorcas.

51

There was nothing Ken could do. He could only watch.

Dorcas had saved him. Not just once, but time and again. Had dragged him unconscious through the most hostile environment, had protected him and provided for his physical and mental safety.

And now that she needed help the most, he could do nothing. Fate was playing a cruel game, making him watch from inches away and making those inches an infinite gap.

Two zombies had made it to the cable. One of them was missing a leg, the other was one that had flayed its way into the tunnel: no skin on its body, just gleaming, seeping muscle and bone.

They oriented themselves, then began sliding toward Dorcas as she hung below them.

"Down, down!" she screamed.

Ken started sliding, but they were on her before he had gone five feet. They were fast, too damn fast.

She screamed again.

"Down, *doowwww….*"

The last word elongated into a shriek of terror. He knew he should keep going, knew that there was nothing he could do for her. But he stopped.

He looked.

She couldn't do much. She only had one good hand, and if she let go of the cable, she could die.

The things seemed to know it, too. Not moving too fast. Taking their time.

Getting into position.

They climbed down the cable, down onto *her*.

Not interested in knocking her off. No, they were going to change her. There was no doubt. As soon as one or the other of them brought its face in range, it would bite her. It would bite her and change her and the warm, brave, *good* woman Ken knew would be gone.

Then there would be three zombies on the cable instead of two.

Ken cursed and began reeling cable between his fingers, letting it pass through his legs. Not knowing how far he had left to go.

Definitely knowing that it didn't matter. Because he only had seconds left. And that wasn't enough time.

The remaining zombies, the ones that still held to the walls of the shaft, resumed their growls. As though urging on the two that were about to add to their ranks.

Hope started cooing again.

Ken looked at her.

She was smiling. She started to laugh.

And as bad as the thought of his own death was, the sound of his little girl laughing as doom poured down on them was infinitely, exquisitely worse.

52

Ken almost let go of the cable as what sounded like a pair of sonic booms exploded through the confined space of the shaft.

Boom.

BOOM.

And then infinite reverberations, echoes that bounced back and forth and up and down and became the entirety of Ken's world for the space of an eternal moment.

He felt dizzy. He closed his eyes. Tried to find his center, tried to regain some semblance of self.

It didn't work.

He opened his eyes and looked up in time to see one of the zombies, one of the things that had been about to bite Dorcas, let go of both her and the cable. It was the legless one, and as it fell Ken saw that it had somehow lost a huge piece of its head as well. Its face had turned inside out, a blasted crevasse ringed by bone and blood.

The back of its head was worse. Just a nub of spine, a bit of hair and skin.

It wasn't dead, though. Of course not. Only *people* died in this horrible reality, this twisted waking nightmare.

The monsters went on forever.

The legless thing fell and disappeared into the darkness of the shaft, spastically clenching its hands and arms, its one leg kicking back and forth.

Ken wondered what would happen once it finally hit bottom.

He wondered if Maggie and Liz and Buck were still alive down there.

He looked up and saw Dorcas still struggling with the other zombie. The one that had no skin, only blood and muscle and bone.

It couldn't bite her, not anymore. Like its legless brother, this zombie had lost most of its head – including its teeth. It had nothing to bite her *with*. But whenever one of these things suffered what should be a killing head trauma, they seemed to go insane. This one was no different.

So it wasn't biting her.

It was beating her to death one-handed.

53

Ken tried to climb. He could have convinced himself that two of the things was too much to handle – especially when all it took was a single bite. But now, watching his friend be pummeled only ten feet above him....

Hearing her scream.

He would hear that scream for the rest of his life if he didn't try to stop the thing from killing her.

But he quickly discovered that wanting to go to Dorcas' rescue was not the same as being able to do it. He still had one hand clamped onto the cable, the other arm dedicated to holding his daughter to him.

He thought for a moment that maybe he could let go and then grab the cable a bit higher and kind of... *lurch* his way up to Dorcas. A bit of wishful thinking that flew in the face of every law of physics.

He actually relaxed his grip for a moment, but the instant his fingers loosened past a certain point, he felt himself start to swing sideways and his hand clenched automatically before he lost his balance and fell away from the cable.

Hope was still laughing. Cackling and clapping as she watched the damaged, maddened zombie pound at Dorcas' arms, trunk, face.

What's wrong with her? What's happening to my daughter?

The other zombies in the shaft were silent again. Crawling around the walls. Skittering almost too quickly to be seen, as though looking for something. Probably searching for a new anchor spot. A new location to begin building another living bridge.

The shaft was nearly silent. Only the suction sounds of the things' hands...

... Dorcas, weeping and praying to God and Jesus and someone to save her save her please *save* her...

... the muffled thud-thumps of the thing as it pounded at her flesh with its own seeping fists...

... and the chirping laughter of Ken's daughter as she watched it all unfold with eyes agleam.

Dorcas gasped and Ken looked up and saw she was about to let go. She couldn't hang on any longer.

She would fall.

And Ken suddenly realized that when that happened she would fall straight down.

Straight into him.

Straight into Hope.

54

"Jesus dear Jesus sweet Jesus please Jesus."

The words were a prayer, but the wet thuds between each one stripped them of their sanctity. The *thwop* of flesh on flesh as the zombie pummeled Dorcas took what should have been a call for heavenly help and converted it to shattered weeping.

The thing hit Dorcas on her already-broken arm.

She screamed.

In Ken's arms, Hope gasped. She sounded like she was on the verge of ecstasy.

Ken closed his eyes. His fingers curled around the greasy cable, the metal fibers biting into his palms and drawing stinging tears from his eyes.

"Oh Jesus please Jesus please –"

"Get offa her!"

Ken's eyes jerked open, his chin snapped up.

The thing was still on Dorcas. One wet hand held to the cable, the other was drawn back, pulled into a tight fist and ready to rain a final blow onto her face. Dorcas was weeping, crying, praying through lips that were bloody and split.

And Aaron flew out of the darkness like vengeance made flesh. He was flipped upside down, his legs twined around the cable, holding his .357 Magnum with his left hand. Smoke poured from the barrel and Ken realized belatedly that that was what must have made the explosions. Aaron had finally used his last two bullets. Had blown the heads off the zombies that were crawling on Dorcas.

Ken had to consciously refrain from shuddering. The cowboy had made the shot in near-perfect darkness, and so far away that Ken couldn't even see him. He had done it hanging upside down, and using his left hand.

And the shots had been perfect. Two head-shots, negating the instant threat, buying Dorcas a few precious seconds.

Ken made a mental note never to get on Aaron's bad side.

Aaron dropped the last few feet and hit the zombie before it could slam its final punch down on Dorcas. The cowboy's gun didn't have any more bullets, but he used it as a combination battering ram/stake, driving the shining barrel into the crater that had once been the monster's head.

Aaron's hand disappeared into the thing's neck. The zombie jerked. Aaron grunted and twisted his arm as it jammed vertically through the zombie's throat.

The zombie made a strange noise, a kind of hiccupping cough. Then it shuddered and fell away from Dorcas, peeling off her like a grotesque second skin.

It fell past Ken and Hope. So close that some of the blood from the thing's peeled flesh wiped across Ken's forearm. It was tacky and surprisingly cool. A breeze followed the thing, and a moment later he heard a thud, then a scream somewhere below him.

"Maggie?" he shouted.

There was no answer.

Dorcas was crying. Shaking so hard that Ken could feel the vibrations in the cable.

He looked back up as Aaron grabbed the cable with his blood-drenched hand and flipped himself over in a move that Ken couldn't even have described, let alone hoped to duplicate. Then the cowboy's legs were wrapped around the cable and he was once again right-side-up, his face only inches from Dorcas'.

"It's okay," said the stocky older man.

Dorcas' eyes were closed, her face a mass of blood and bruising. Aaron used his right sleeve to mop some of the blood from her face. "It's okay," he said again, his voice so low Ken could barely here it. "I gotcha, girl."

Dorcas nodded. She was sobbing. But the sobs slowed a bit when Aaron put his arm around her. And slowed still more when he said, "Let's get outta this damn place."

It grew brighter as he spoke. Christopher was coming down.

"Did I miss anything?" he hollered.

Dorcas started laughing. Still crying, but laughing as well, as though refusing to let distress claim her completely. Refusing to be cowed.

"Not much," she managed a second later. She looked down at Ken. "Don't just hang there staring up my petticoats. Get a move on!"

Ken nodded. He started down again.

And tried not to think about the zombies he saw a few feet above Christopher, clinging to each other, clinging to the wall.

Building another bridge.

55

Hope stopped laughing.

"You okay, Hope?" Ken said. He didn't stop descending. Just kept letting the cable slide through his grease- and blood-soaked palm. Kept letting himself drop foot by aching foot into the black.

Hope didn't answer.

He spared a glance at her. She was staring up at nothing.

He didn't know what to do for her. She hadn't been bitten. She *couldn't* have been. If she had been bitten, she would have changed already. She wouldn't be Hope, she would be dead and gone, just a corpse that hadn't been buried.

But *something* was happening to her.

And there's nothing you can do about it now. So just move.

He dropped through infinity. Wondering if his descent would ever end, or if the change that had come over the earth had also changed the elevator shaft. What if it went on forever? What if it just kept going until Ken and the rest of the survivors found themselves in the deepest pits of Hell?

We're already there.

And there was truth in that.

Derek was gone, after all. His son was gone. His wife was somewhere beyond his reach, his baby girl with her.

And his daughter… what was happening to Hope?

She was cooing again. And he felt something in the cable. A shiver. A tremble.

"Guys." Christopher's voice floated down from above, the tones of a strangely lighthearted oracle. "We should hurry."

And the way he said it told Ken why Hope was cooing. She had sensed it before anyone.

The zombies had bridged to the cable again. And there was no way to knock more debris down on them.

The vibrations in the cable became more pronounced, and it wasn't hard for Ken to imagine the hands and feet gripping the metal fibers, slipping down hand over hand. Skinless fingers feeling their way down in the dark, questing for helpless prey.

"Faster," someone whispered from above. Ken couldn't tell who it was.

He opened his grip on the cable. Opened it until he was nearly falling. Preferring to die on impact than be captured by the things above him.

The air whipped past his ears, whistling and whining.

But it couldn't hide the sound of growls above.

Or the sound of his daughter sighing and giggling in his arms.

"Yes," she whispered. *"Yesssssss."*

56

Ken hit something. His left foot hit first, and a bolt of pain seared through his toes, his ankle, his shin, his thigh bone. His hip almost buckled under him.

He had fallen too many times today. He had twisted his back. He didn't know what it was, exactly, but there was something going wrong inside him.

He stumbled back, off-balance.

It registered – albeit dimly – that there was something to stumble back *on*. That he was on some kind of flooring. *Terra firma.*

Then his heel collided with something hard. His left heel, of course. New pain rocketed up to his back. He screamed.

Hope giggled.

He realized he had let go of the elevator cable. He probably would have let go of Hope, too, if she hadn't been more or less attached to him with his belt.

He tripped over whatever it was, falling backward in a series of jumbled half-steps that took him away from the cable, away from the only tether he had had on location or direction.

His right foot went behind him, a reverse lunge step. Too far for comfort, and the agony in his back increased.

His foot came down on nothing. Nothing at all. Just dark, empty air.

Ken had a panicked moment to wonder what was happening. A terrified instant to realize that he must have reached the bottom of the elevator cable. To then understand that the logical thing at the bottom of an elevator cable would be the elevator itself.

And that he was about to fall of the side of it.

Hope clapped gleefully in the dark. Laughing as Ken pitched into nothing.

57

The fall was short.

Less than a few inches. And it came with a tearing sound.

Someone grunted.

"Help me, you idiot."

Ken didn't recognize the voice. It wasn't one of the survivors, one of *his* people.

Then he saw the form in the darkness, huge and black. Fear rippled through him for a moment, joining the pain in his back and leg and creating a strangely discordant harmony of terror and agony.

"Help... me...."

Ken felt himself slipping backward. Downward. The dark figure moved toward him.

He finally realized who it was. It was Buck. The big man had caught Ken's shirt sleeve. The shirt – the ridiculous long-sleeve thing that said "I went to BOISE and all I got was this STUPID SHIRT (and a raging case of *the CLAP*)." that Ken had gotten from a dead man – was not designed to bear a person's body weight, and it was tearing. He could hear it ripping at the seams, pulling away from him.

And then what?

Ken grabbed for Buck's shaded form. The other man grunted as Ken accidentally flailed and hit him a half-dozen times him before finally managing to get a good grip on his arm. Buck backed up slowly, and Ken felt himself drawn back to the top of the elevator car.

He made it all of two steps before kicking something else and tripping. At least this time he tripped forward.

"Jesus," snapped Buck. "Can't you stand up straight?"

"Sorry," Ken mumbled. Then he screamed as pain lanced through his ankle. Not nerve pain, not whatever was wrong with his back and left leg. In fact, this wasn't his left leg at all.

It was his right leg. His right ankle.

He looked down.

And screamed again. Not merely in pain, not merely in horror. This time it was revulsion and a sense that right and wrong had abandoned themselves, that madness reigned supreme.

The zombies that had bridged to the cable had been shattered. They had been broken. But they had not been destroyed. And the proof was all around him. The proof was at his feet. The proof held tight *to* his foot.

A hand had somehow grabbed his ankle. The hand led to a forearm, but the forearm did not in turn lead to anything else. It simply *ended*.

Ken flashed to watching Thing on reruns of *The Addams Family*. The disembodied hand skittered around and caused mischief wherever it went. A ridiculous sight gag made even more ridiculous by what passed for special effects back then.

But what held onto Ken's leg was no special effect. It was real. And holding so tightly he could already feel his foot going numb. Blood started to seep around the hand as the pressure of the grip started to shear Ken's skin away from his flesh.

His knees buckled and he almost went down. Stopped himself.

Next to him was a head. A still-moving head. Eyes staring in rage. Mouth opening and closing.

What if he had fallen on it?

What if it bit him?

He reeled back. Felt gorge rising in his throat.

Buck grunted. He shuffled forward and punted the decapitated head like a football, kicking it off the side of the elevator before kneeling next to Ken and ripping the hand away in one brute motion. Ken yelled as the hand tore more skin from his already-lacerated flesh.

"Come on," said Buck.

Ken nodded. Tried not to notice how much of the top of the elevator was moving.

Failed.

58

Ken only took a single step before he asked, "Where's Maggie?"

"Who's Maggie?"

A double-thud interrupted them. Ken saw two bodies, nearly intertwined, land on the elevator. Dorcas and Aaron. The cowboy still had his arm around Dorcas, and seemed hesitant to let go of her even when they had both feet on the solid platform of the elevator.

"Move, move, move!"

The light grew brighter around them. Ken looked up.

Christopher was a few feet above. Coming down fast.

And behind him, it looked like the darkness itself had come alive.

59

Ken had seen Christopher climb through places he would have thought were inaccessible. The kid was a born daredevil, a combination of adrenaline junky and natural ability.

But he was losing ground to the teeming mass of things that clambered over each other as they climbed down the cable behind him.

Ken looked at Buck. Even in the dim light of Christopher's flashlight, he could see the big man pale visibly.

"Come on," said Buck.

He yanked Ken – still stumbling – over the uneven mass of machinery and broken cables that comprised the top of the elevator car. And now that the light had grown a bit brighter, Ken could also see how close he had come to pitching off the side and into nothing. They were nowhere near the bottom of the shaft. It had to be at least another five or six floors to the ground, and who knew what that would even look like?

Buck had saved him.

And now the big man was leading him to a dark gap in the top of the elevator.

"Emergency hatch," said Buck, seeming to key off Ken's look.

Ken hesitated. When a horde of monsters was on your trail, going into a windowless box didn't seem like the wisest course.

"Get in," said Buck.

"Are you nuts?" said Aaron behind them.

Ken looked over his shoulder. The cowboy was casting about, looking for alternate escape routes.

"There's *nowhere else*," said Buck. His voice rose to a screech, half pleading, half enraged. Then he shook his head as though resigned. "Fine, do what you want."

He moved to the hatch and squatted beside it. Then looked at Ken. "But your wife is in here."

Then he dropped down and disappeared into the black square.

60

Ken's feet started moving the second he heard Buck say Maggie was in the elevator. It didn't even occur to him that the man might be lying. Not until he was bent over the darkness, looking down and wondering what the best way would be to get in.

Alive. She's alive.

He sat on the edge of the hatchway, dangling his legs into darkness. Even knowing Mags was down there, it made his skin crawl to see himself disappear so suddenly and completely.

We're all going to die.

Unless we give up.

Give in.

Ken realized that he was hearing the growling from the things above. That his thoughts were somehow being coopted by the zombies' hypnotic howls and rumbles. But it didn't matter.

He didn't want to go down there. Not into the darker dark. Not now.

Give up.

He felt something warm at his cheek. Hope had laid her head on his chest, looking up at him – or at the things coming down the cable – and she was moaning, her breath warm on his face. An unnerving smile on her small features. She looked sad and hungry and hopeful and gleeful and afraid all at once.

"Dammit."

Ken saw Aaron kick something over the side of the elevator. A twitching thing that could have been an arm or a leg and that in any just and right world should not have moved at all. The cowboy turned to look at Dorcas, who was staring at him.

"Buck was right. Nowhere else to go."

"I don't want to –" Dorcas began.

Aaron shook his head. Looked up, then grabbed her around the shoulders and hustled her the few steps across the top of the elevator.

"We don't have a choice."

Give up.

Give in.

Give up.

Give in.

The elevator shook as Christopher touched down.

Ken pushed himself off the edge of the hatchway. He fell into darkness once more. Landed and took a stumbling step away, thinking dimly that he had to get out of the way before the others came in.

He was right. He barely moved out of the way before another black figure came into the cab. The form didn't fall, but was lowered by one arm. Dorcas.

Aaron followed, jumping easily to the floor, his cowboy boots thudding as he landed.

Only Christopher left. And as the young man started to lower himself in Ken realized:

Who would close the escape door? It wouldn't do much good to run in here and then leave a clear opening for the things to follow.

"Wait —" he began.

Too late.

Christopher dropped in with a grunt. A thick clunk followed him almost instantly: the sound of metal clacking against metal, of wood and plastic bouncing up and then settling down again just as fast.

He pulled it shut. He pulled the hatch shut.

Ken didn't feel like rejoicing, though. Because the things that were following the young man had already shown an ability to get through doors. What about closed hatches?

Was it even locked?

Christopher landed in a crouch, still holding Buck's LED light. He straightened and turned around quickly, illuminating the other survivors.

And Ken finally saw Maggie. She stood beside the closed doors of the elevator, leaning over and around the still-slumped form of Liz. The toddler's skin looked pale and waxy, and Ken feared the worst. Then he saw a thin stream of spit spill out of his baby's mouth, catching the light for an instant before it broke off and hit the floor.

He'd never been so happy to see one of his children drooling. Because the dead didn't produce saliva, did they?

"Maggie," he said. He supposed he should have shouted it, should have screamed it and leaped across the cab to her. But the word was barely a whisper, and he didn't move at all.

He was afraid she wasn't real.

He was afraid he was seeing, not a woman, but a memory. A hope of something gone.

Maggie turned her head. She didn't look happy to see him; barely looked at him at all. She looked at Buck. "It won't open," she said.

"Maggie." This time he said it a little louder. He managed to take a step toward her, and reached for her.

"Don't touch me." She didn't scream. A scream would have been better. A scream would have splashed all over the inside of the elevator, would have hit everything and everyone and maybe spread some of the venom around. Instead, the words seemed to hit Ken square in the face. He felt like he'd been punched, or like someone had taken a hammer to the bridge of his nose.

Total silence reigned. No one seemed to breathe, as though all that had come before was merely a precursor, a curtain call to this main event.

Ken knew what was happening. You didn't stay happily married for as long as he had without understanding your spouse. You didn't understand your spouse without seeing the things they loved. And you didn't see the things they loved without understanding their deepest fears.

She had seen Derek fall.

She had seen Derek change.

And it didn't matter that it hadn't been Ken's fault. That there was nothing he could have done. That Derek had done it himself in a stunning display of selfless courage. She couldn't blame Derek for what had happened. You didn't blame the hero for the loss. And the girls… too young to bear responsibility for what happened to Derek.

So that left Ken.

He wondered for a moment if his marriage was over. If the Armageddon that had killed so much of the world had also murdered his marriage. And wondered if that would render his life worthless. So much of who he now was began with the words husband and father.

What if half of that was gone?

Maggie's face was phasing through a series of emotions, none of them good. Distrust, anger, confusion, fear, sorrow. All of them seeming like sharp knives cast directly at him.

Then Maggie seemed to notice Hope. The little girl was still keening. Almost singing wordlessly from her perch on Ken's chest. Reaching toward the ceiling, staring up with fever-bright eyes that did not notice or did not care to see her mother only a few short feet away.

"What's wrong with her?" Maggie said. It was almost a whimper, the venom gone from her voice as fast as it had come. Now there was only fear. Terror that bit as deeply and painfully as had the hate.

"I don't know." His words sounded empty. Sounded like the worst kind of lie: the truth of helpless despair.

Give up.

Give in.

Ken stepped toward Maggie. He felt like if he could hold her, could even touch her hand, they could fix this. They could get through this.

He knew they could survive as long as the family remained. Derek was gone, but they could endure. The family could ride out the storm.

Something hit the top of the elevator. Then something else. Then the whole cab shook as what sounded like a hundred feet pounded across the ceiling.

A moment later, the strange sucking noises Ken had heard before oozed their way into the elevator, and thumps and thuds resounded through the walls of the suspended cage that had become their world.

And then noises came through the floor.

The things were crawling on the walls. Everywhere. Above, below, around them.

Something coughed outside the elevator. A gagging, choking noise that made Ken's hackles rise, because he knew what it meant.

Smoke started seeping in through one of the corners of the elevator where the back wall met the ceiling.

Something else coughed. More smoke, this time coming from the floor.

"They're gonna burn their way in," said Dorcas.

"Or just burn *us*," said Christopher.

61

Buck was on the door in an instant. "Move!" he yelled. He shoved Maggie out of the way, and Ken saw Liz's head snap to the side as his wife was pushed with her oh-so-precious cargo.

"Hey!" shouted Ken. He jumped at Buck. Not really knowing what he was going to do, only knowing that the man had lain hands on his wife, had bounced his baby girl around like she was less important than a sack of flour.

He thought he might be able to kill the man. He wondered for an instant if the only monsters were the ones outside the elevator.

The floor lurched. Not just a little, either. Ken's feet almost went out from under him as the world suddenly tilted to the right, to the left. Then dropped a good six inches.

Screams. Everyone in the elevator seemed to be hollering at once, either in panic or trying to stop others *from* panicking.

"We're gonna fall!" Christopher.

"Oh, Jesus, please!" Dorcas.

"Someone help me get this damn door open!" Buck.

"Kenny!" Maggie.

"Everyone *shut up*!" Aaron.

And his voice did it. He was standing in the back corner of the elevator, the only one who seemed to be unaffected by the sudden jouncing. "The elevator won't fall."

"What if the cable breaks?" Buck again. He was scrabbling at the doors with his fingers, and Ken could see dark streaks on the burnished metal. Blood. The man had already broken his skin and nails, clawing at a door that wouldn't open.

We're going to die here.

"The cable don't matter," said Aaron. "There's electromagnetic brakes on the rails."

Buck hesitated for a moment in his panic-scratching. Turned and stared at Aaron in amazement, as though he had just found the blue-ribbon winner in the idiot contest. "Electromagnets don't work when the power's out, you *dumb shit.*"

Aaron's jaw clenched. In a low voice he said, "The electromagnets keep the brakes *open.* So when the power goes out, they clamp down. No power, no falling." He took a step toward Buck. "And you need to calm down or I will calm you down. Forcefully."

Buck looked like he was going to rise to the threat, but instead he doubled over in a coughing fit. Smoke had saturated the elevator cab. Ken's eyes were watering, and the light in Christopher's hand was being dampened by a greasy yellow-gray smog.

Buck straightened. "Don't..." (coughing) "... tell me to...."

He couldn't finish.

Ken saw something. He didn't recognize it at first. And then recognized it, but couldn't believe it.

He had seen the zombies vomiting acid. The bilious stuff was black and thick, a tarry fluid that melted through metal and concrete and wood with equal ease.

But that was what he had seen in the light of day.

Here, in the gloom of the dark and smoke-filled cab, Ken saw a dot of light on the ceiling, a purplish glint that reminded him of the black lights the DJs used for some of the high school dances –

(*Only there's no more high school, there's no more* world, *for crying out loud.*)

– or at some of the clubs he and Maggie used to go to. Smoke roiled around it, and a low sizzling skittered through the cab. The acid glowed. It burned, both inside and outside. But the light it brought was cold. Cold light that burned. Beautiful color that would kill.

The sight of it made discordant bells go off in Ken's head.

The glowing drop of acid finished searing its way through the ceiling tiles. It rolled into a ball and began to elongate, an oval pearl extending into the cab right above Buck's head.

Ken grabbed the big man and yanked him over. Hope squealed as she was pancaked between the two of them, but Ken didn't have time to worry about whether he had frightened her, or if she was even reacting to this or to some other, unseen stimulus.

"What the hell are –" Buck fell on top of Ken, but stopped speaking when he saw the acid fall to the floor and start sizzling through the spot where he had been standing.

Everyone moved instinctively to the sides of the cab.

Ken cast his eyes around. Looking for Maggie. Caught her glance, saw the terror in her eyes.

The car lurched again. He wondered how many of the things were on the walls and ceiling of the elevator, how many were clinging below the floor. How many would it hold? Surely the brakes would have to give out eventually.

So would they fall to their deaths?

Be asphyxiated by the smoke?

Or be burnt by the acid?

He looked at Buck. The man was shaking. "The doors won't open," the big man said. He sounded like he wanted to add the words, "I want my mommy." Instead he simply repeated, "The doors won't open."

And Ken saw more acid – not a drop this time but a stream – gathering on a crack in the ceiling directly above him.

62

A scream pulled Ken's attention away from the beading string of glowing liquid above him.

It was Aaron. Not just screaming now, but shrieking. And coming from the unflappable cowboy the sound was nearly as out of place as the sight of the disembodied hand that had gripped Ken's leg earlier.

Still howling, Aaron shook his left arm, then slammed into the wall of the elevator, not seeming to mind that he hit his dislocated and broken fingers into the wall.

Ken had seen a rabid animal once. A wolf. He was eleven, hiking a trail near Caldwell with his Webelos Scout den. It was late fall, and an early snow had already fallen. Some of the parents wanted to cancel the hike, but the Den Mother, a woman named Mrs. Prescott who Ken remembered as being lanky and so strong she could probably bench press God, had successfully argued that the drive to Caldwell would probably be the most dangerous part of the trip.

She was mostly right. The hike was nice. Snow frosted the evergreens that anchored the edges of the trail, but little of it was on the trail itself. The scouts were bundled up in layers of clothes and most had thermoses of hot chocolate in their coats. It was fun. Just enough snow to make a snowball from time to time, not enough to make it miserable.

Ken had run ahead to avoid being hit by a snowball, in fact, when the saw the wolf. He ran around a sharp curve in the trail and saw the beast. It wasn't doing anything. Just standing there. Its fur was black with white spots, its muzzle streaked with flecks of froth and blood.

Ken froze. The wolf didn't seem to notice him at first. It was biting its own leg. Then it spun around three times, chasing not its tail but nothing at all.

Mrs. Prescott came around the corner next. The wolf noticed Ken now. It growled, drawing its muzzle back to show teeth so long and sharp that Ken thought he was going to faint dead away.

The wolf jumped at him. And Mrs. Prescott proved to be not only strong, but a believer in concealed carry laws. She pulled a gun out from under her jacket and pulled the trigger and put a single shot right through the wolf's right cheek.

The wolf flopped at Ken's feet. He screamed and cried. Mrs. Prescott held him and rocked him and told the other Den Mother – Ken could never remember her name – to take the boys back to the cars while she waited next to the wolf's body until someone could call in the shot and get the thing hauled off for testing.

Ken didn't go back to scouts much after that. But he remembered the look in the wolf's eyes when it jumped. That mad, lost look.

And that was what he was seeing in Aaron. Pain and a need to do the irrational that was so deep-seated it became sublime.

The cowboy rammed himself into the wall. Again and again. Then began rubbing the left side of his body against the wall, writhing against it like he was trying out for a job as the world's worst exotic dancer.

And still screaming.

"He's changing," said Christopher, shrinking away from Aaron.

Then Aaron charged at Ken.

63

Ken was still on the floor, still half-pinned by Buck's larger form. He couldn't move couldn't move *couldn't move*.

And even if he *had* been able to move... where would he have gone?

They were all stuck. Trapped.

Aaron rushed across the elevator. It was large, perhaps a freight elevator. Something used to haul up large furniture or machinery. Things the building management wouldn't want the tenants to see on a regular basis.

Thank goodness, at least we'll die discretely.

Not a huge consolation. Ken had a second to remember Aaron wading into a stairwell full of zombies – and somehow emerging with only a few broken fingers – before the cowboy's deadly hands reached for him.

He shouted. Tried to scramble away.

"Ken!" screamed Maggie.

"Don't!" yelled Dorcas.

Aaron ignored them both. Smoke seemed to be pouring from his body, transforming him into a monster.

Buck lurched. "Leave them alone," said the man. His voice cracked. But he tried to get between Aaron and Ken. Or maybe between Aaron and Hope, who was suddenly silent.

Either way, Aaron smashed a fist into Buck's chin, sending the big man rolling into the elevator doors, crashing into Maggie's legs. He lay there and coughed and spat blood.

Aaron grabbed Ken.

Ken tried to get his hands up. He had fought before. He had taken martial arts his entire life. He should be able to do something. Anything.

He made a fist.

Aaron slapped his balled-up hand away.

Punched his throat.

And suddenly, Ken couldn't breathe.

64

This is how you die. The world doesn't explode. The monsters don't kill you. It's a crazy cowboy karate-chopping your throat.

The thoughts bounced around in Ken's head like BBs in a blender. He felt like he was overheating. Could practically *hear* himself overheating.

But that was wrong, wasn't it?

Shouldn't he be going numb?

Shouldn't he be dying... faster?

He realized Aaron was shaking him. Yelling. Not screaming, not shrieking. Yelling. Words.

"Stop trying to hit me, ya crazy kid!"

And Ken realized that he was still pummeling at Aaron with his good hand, still had his bad hand wrapped as much as possible around Hope, pinning her to him. She was silent, head down on his chest like she was looking forward to hearing the last beats of his heart.

Aaron batted Ken's hand away again, and his face screwed up in a scowl. "Quit it or I'll crack you in the throat again."

That penetrated the fog that had invaded Ken's brain. He also realized he was breathing. Not dead at all. Somehow alive, somehow still breathing.

His throat hurt like hell.

"Why'd you...." His voice sounded like a combination of rusty nails and chunks of dirt. He hacked. Tried again. "Why'd you hit me."

"'Cause you weren't gonna move and I didn't have time to chat."

Aaron looked up. Then down.

Ken followed his gaze. Gulped. "Thank you," he said. His voice came out as a murmur, and this time it had nothing to do with his bruised vocal cords. "Thank you."

"Welcome." Aaron looked again at the hole where the acid had eaten through the ceiling, and the matching hole in the floor where Ken's head had been a moment before. "Don't imagine you'd have liked that."

"I thought...." Ken coughed. The sound was louder than he expected. He realized it was silent in the cab. "I thought you were changing."

"Why would you think *that*?" Aaron seemed torn between amusement and offense.

"You went all crazy."

Aaron showed him his left arm. A long line of black, charred flesh ran from his shoulder to his elbow. "Some of that goo hit me. Just a drop, and it did this." He shuddered. "Never felt anything like that. And I been through some things."

The elevator pitched again, falling a few inches.

"We can't stay here," Dorcas whispered.

"How do we get out?" said Christopher. The two of them were in the far corner, nearly holding one another as though they had taken refuge in each other's arms when Aaron had gone crazy.

"The doors won't open. They're stuck," said Buck, rolling over and clutching his nose. Blood streamed from his fingers and spattered the floor.

Ken realized something in that instant.

He had thought before that it was silent in the car. He was wrong. It wasn't silent in the car. It was silent *outside*.

In the next moment, Hope sighed. Ken looked at his daughter. She was grinning in a way he had never seen. An old smile, the smile not of an innocent child, but of someone who has seen far too many things that are far too dark.

She *winked*.

And outside the car, several coughs sounded.

Acid sizzled. Not randomly, but directly above Buck's head, above Dorcas and Christopher, above Ken and Aaron.

The things outside had found a way to target them.

65

Everyone moved.

Ken tried to roll away. Got tangled in himself. He heard the *sssss-hissss* of acid above him.

Feet pounded on the floor.

He grunted. Rolled on his bad hand. The stumps of his missing fingers scraped on the floor. He almost screamed, but something stopped him. He bit his tongue and the inside of his cheek. The new pain drew his mind away from the red bloom of agony centered at the stumps of his missing fingers.

Hope was still smiling. Grinning.

How do they know where we are?

The thought entered his mind that they knew because Hope was here. That they knew because *she* knew.

She was wrapped in that crap for hours.

What if they did something to her?

What if they changed her somehow? Made her one of them? A spy? What if they see whatever she sees?

No. That's impossible.

Of course, everything else that had happened in these hours was impossible as well. Why not one more thing?

And the answer was simple: if the things knew everything they were doing, then there was no hope of escape. So that *couldn't* be the answer. Because it would be a useless answer. And Ken wouldn't accept a solution that ended with his family and the rest of the survivors – the rest of *humanity* – doomed.

So no. Not some kind of telepathy.

What else?

He tried to get to his feet. Hope's weight on his chest, her body dragging at the belt that cinched them both together, pulled him off-center. He almost fell again. His good hand went down on the floor. Fingers plunged into nothing.

There was a hole there.

Something grabbed his fingers.

He pulled them back, terror wringing a curse from his lips. The things were underneath. Waiting for someone to put a hand through the floor, perhaps? Just waiting to bite?

What would happen if someone changed in here?

The answer was a nightmare movie that played out quickly in his mind.

He realized the others were screaming as they moved away from the acid that hissed through the ceiling. Realized that everyone was making noise. Too much noise to think.

Buck's foot went through a hole in the floor. He yelled and yanked it out, and Ken saw fingers clutching at the man's heel.

Maggie cried out in terror.

Dorcas hollered as Christopher was almost splattered by a stream of acid that fell from above, then splashed against a wall that hissed and started to dissolve.

Smoke.

Coughing.

Screaming.

Too much noise.

Can't think.

Too much.

And Ken suddenly understood.

The elevator fell another three inches. More.

Screams.

He didn't know if they would have enough time to get out. The things outside were too many and too heavy. The brakes must be shot.

They were going to fall.

66

"Shut up!"

Ken's shout worked, though probably more because they were surprised at the outburst than because of any inherent power in his still-gravelly voice. Everyone fell silent. Trying to split glances between him, the sizzling ceiling tiles, and the spots that were gradually opening in the floor.

He gestured them to move toward the center of the cab. Finger over his lips.

It had been silent.

Hope had been silent.

She had been cooing and calling on the cables. And even in the elevator for a few moments.

Then she stopped.

Why?

And Ken had thought that it was quiet for a moment in the cab, but he was wrong. It had been quiet *outside*. The things, the growling, snuffling, snarling things, had been *silent*.

He remembered the ones that bounded over the bridge of their fellows. The ones with eyes covered. Blind, but not falling.

Chirping.

And the acid falling from the ceiling. Vomited forth after each of them screamed, or spoke.

They were *listening*. The monsters were hearing. Targeting them like sub-killers looking for U-boats. Dropping acid instead of depth charges, but the idea was the same.

Silence was salvation.

Ken pulled everyone together.

The sizzle-spit-crackle of burning acid was the only sound.

The elevator cracked. Plunged a full foot. Christopher inhaled, and Ken wondered if the young man was going to scream and kill them all.

Dorcas slammed her hand over his mouth. She nodded at Ken. She understood.

They stood in a tight circle.

Waiting.

The elevator creaked around them.

What now?

67

Hope was staring at him.

Liz still dangled from the carrier on Maggie's chest. Ken wondered if it was better this way. He didn't know if he would be able to deal with it if she opened her eyes and stared at him with that same knowing gaze, or gave him the same grin that Hope kept turning on him.

He looked away from her. Back at Maggie. Her eyes flitted to his eyes, then away, to his eyes, then away. Not looking at anything else, but not able to face him for long, either.

We're in trouble.

He knew it wasn't just the elevator, either. Wasn't just now. It was Derek. It was losing their son.

He was the father. He was the protector. The one thing he was supposed to do was keep his family alive.

And he had failed.

He turned to the front of the elevator. More to avoid having to look at Maggie than for any concrete reason, but as he turned he thought of something.

They're not smart.

Yes, they are.

But not smarter than us.

He went to the doors. Careful to avoid putting his foot through the hole that Buck had nearly plunged his own leg through a moment before. The doors were open a quarter-inch. Enough to wedge his fingertips between. No more. He pulled with his good hand.

No give.

He cast his eyes at Buck. The big man was gazing at him with an "I told you so" look, large arms crossed over his chest.

Ken nodded for him to join him at the front of the cab. Buck hesitated as though deciding how much of a fuss to put up. Then he seemed to remember they were all in this together.

He came to Ken's side. "They won't move." He whispered the words.

Ken looked up. Waited for a cough. For acid to rain on them. Nothing.

He looked back at Buck. "Pull them," he whispered.

"Didn't you hear me?"

"Just do it."

Buck sighed. He couldn't fit his fingers in the crack. Just lay the bloody pads of his fingers against the edges of the door and began scrabbling.

Ken took a deep breath.

And began making noise.

68

Buck stared at Ken in horror, and stopped pulling for a moment.

Two hands stabbed out and took his place. Christopher. Grin back in its normal position, his fingers darting into the crack and pulling for all he was worth as Ken continued banging away at the door.

Whud... whud... whud....

The sound of his fist thumping against the door sounded not merely loud, but deafening in the space. The crackle of burning floor and ceiling tiles was the only other noise, an eerie and almost painful crepitation that crawled through the empty spaces in the cab like a many-legged insect.

Whud... whud....

Something coughed above him.

Not directly above, I hope.

He looked down. Hope was still staring at him. Not smiling, not looking with that too-knowing gaze. She appeared almost confused, and Ken chose to take that as a good sign.

He kept hammering at the door. Three more hits.

Another cough. Gagging and rasping. The first time he had seen one of the things vomit the acid, the stuff had melted its own flesh. He wondered if that would happen every time; if the things would have to essentially suicide to produce this weapon.

That's assuming they're not already dead.

The world had gone insane hours ago. The pre-change rules no longer applied.

The sound of sizzling, the acid-smell of charring plastic and metal drew Ken's attention outward.

He looked up. Waiting for the glowing appearance of the acid. Expecting it to fall through the ceiling, to splash over his face, to burn through his skull and fry his brain to mush.

Nothing.

Something else was happening, though.

"You feel that?" whispered Christopher.

Ken nodded. And banged harder.

69

"It's starting to hurt!"

"I know!"

"Really!"

"I know!"

Ken was aware they were no longer whispering. But he didn't care. He couldn't let it stop him. He kept hitting the door. Kept pounding at it – with both fists now, even though each hit with his maimed left hand sent shockwaves of pain through his entire body.

The things were moving again. They sounded surprisingly light, a soughing of leaves overhead, a sighing of wind to the sides and beneath their feet.

Then more gagging, more coughing. More sizzling.

More heat.

The elevator doors were starting to get hot to the touch. Ken had gambled that the things were following the sounds the survivors were making. Had hoped that if he hit the doors, the monsters would spew acid on them – behind them – and maybe melt whatever was holding them locked in place.

So far it hadn't worked. The zombies weren't puking acid directly on their heads, true, so that much had worked out. But the doors were still solidly shut. And getting hot. Acid must be waterfalling its way down the other side of the metal. Eating through from that side.

The elevator began sliding down.

Ken looked at Aaron. The cowboy shook his head. Just an inch to the left, an inch to the right, but it was enough to communicate that whatever brakes had been holding the elevator aloft were giving out.

Christopher was groaning. A low, animal moan. Pain. But he didn't stop pulling the doors.

Buck started pulling as well. Shouldered Ken aside and yanked on the doors.

Something inside the mechanism pinged.

The doors slid open a few inches.

Far enough to allow one of the zombies – one that had climbed down from the elevator, perhaps, or maybe one that had been looking through the building proper for them – to heave itself into the elevator.

70

The thing lurched forward, and Ken saw Christopher fling himself back. He didn't shout.

No one did.

It was as though the cab was no longer filled with the living, but with the dead. With ghosts who were only going through the motions of life, but stripped of all voice.

Buck didn't move away.

He grabbed a hank of the zombie's hair. Slammed the thing's head sideways into the acid-heated elevator doors. Flesh bubbled and the zombie screamed.

Ken moved forward, not sure what he was going to do, but sure he couldn't let the thing get into the cab. Sure he couldn't let it bite Buck.

The elevator fell. Not a small drop this time. Probably ten feet. Everyone tumbled to the floor.

And still not a sound.

Not even when Buck managed to stand and Ken realized the big man was still holding onto the zombie's hair. Still holding the thing's snapping head at bay... even though the head was no longer attached to anything else. The body had been left behind, neatly decapitated by the ceiling as the elevator fell.

Buck held the head at arm's length, his face almost comically disgusted. The zombie's teeth opened and closed, its teeth clapping and gnashing. No sound came from its mouth.

Not breathing.

No heart.

As Ken watched, the stump of the neck started to froth. Bone and blood and muscle disappeared, sealed over by a waxy yellow substance that reminded him of the stuff the zombies had been secreting in the building where he found his family.

Before Derek died.

Don't think that.

What the hell is HAPPENING?

The frothing stopped. The zombie's eyes rolled around, looking from one person in the cab to another. It was still silent, but its teeth kept snapping.

Ken heard someone gag. Sounded like Maggie.

"Guys!"

Ken tore his eyes from the horrific, impossible vision of death that refused to die.

Christopher had stood up. Was staring at something. But before Ken could do more than glance at it, the coughing started again. From everywhere.

71

Ken grabbed Maggie. She didn't pull away from him this time, didn't make any pretense of resistance. She was almost limp, like the sight of the thing that still spit and bit while held aloft by nothing more than Buck's hand had burned out any resentment she held against Ken.

He shoved her toward Christopher. The younger man caught her and started moving Ken's wife toward the gap in the elevator doors. Toward the gap in the outer doors that led to a dark floor beyond.

There was an offset between the level of the elevator and the level of the floor past it. Not only that, but the outer doors were only open about a foot and a half. Ken couldn't tell what had opened them, but he wasn't about to question one of the rare gifts received in all this. Still, the gap was only barely wide enough to allow his wife to exit, shimmying through with Liz at her chest, stepping up to get to the floor that was about a foot above the floor of the elevator.

And then she was gone. Disappeared in the darkness.

Ken turned around. "Dorcas!"

The older woman moved forward. She glanced at Aaron as though hesitant to leave without him. He nodded and gave her a swift shove.

She pushed her way through the gap as well.

Followed by Aaron.

Then Christopher.

Buck didn't move through it all. Just stared at the head. He looked like the sight of it had frozen something in him, had sent his mind into a fractal freefall that would permit no escape.

"Buck." Buck didn't move.

Ken realized he shouldn't have been able to see anything. Christopher was gone, and with him the light.

He looked up.

The entire ceiling was aglow. Bulging and curving. Acid ready to fall through not in a trickle or a stream, but in a torrent. A waterfall that would doom anyone inside the elevator.

"Buck, we have to go. Now!"

Buck didn't seem to hear him. Ken tried pulling the big man. Nothing.

He moved to the gap. "Buck, please!" he called, but he couldn't stay. Not any longer.

He stepped into the gap. Stepped through and up to the floor beyond. Halfway between worlds. Between one Hell and, perhaps, another.

But at least Maggie was waiting on the floor.

He stepped up. Leading with Hope. Half his body in the elevator. Half his body out.

And something grabbed his hair.

72

A scream tore its way out of Ken's throat. Not just fear, but indignation. He was halfway out of the elevator, halfway back to being *alive*, dammit. What was stopping him?

At first he thought it was Buck. But why would the big man grab him?

Besides, the angle was wrong. This was something else.

The growling started again. Snarling. The ugly and yet subtly hypnotic call of the monsters, and Ken felt himself drawn upwards. He rose to the balls of his feet and realized that one of the things on top of the elevator must have reached down somehow, must have caught him.

Something blinded him. A bouncing light that seemed far too bright and also made his skin crawl, as though the terror that held him tight had also given him temporary synesthesia. He could feel sights and hear colors and smell tastes and everything was mixed up in his mind and he wondered –

(*Is this what it feels like before you die?*)

– what was happening.

Something tore Hope away from him. He screamed. Reached for her. The thing slapped his hand down. "Stop!" shouted a voice.

Christopher. The light Ken was seeing was the penlight the younger man had appropriated from Buck. And now Christopher was yanking at him. Trying to pull Ken the rest of the way out of the elevator.

But the thing above wouldn't let go. Ken felt his neck popping. Felt like his head would be yanked free from his shoulders.

Smoke poured out of the elevator around him.

The elevator jounced again. Dropped another inch. Ken saw an image of Buck holding the decapitated head. Wondered if he would be severed so cleanly in half along his vertical axis.

No, it'll be messier.

Christopher pulled harder. So did the thing on top.

The elevator was groaning and moaning like a living thing about to give in to a fatal wound.

And then something hit Ken on the back of the head.

73

Where a moment before Christopher's light had blinded Ken, now he could barely see it. His vision blurred, then doubled momentarily. He blinked, tried to shake his head. Couldn't.

What's —

Why can't —

Something's got me.

The jumble of thoughts resorted themselves just in time for something to hit him again. Christopher was pulling him forward, the monster that had reached down from on top of the elevator was pulling him up. The elevator was about to fall.

And *whump*.

Ken's vision didn't blur this time, but rather exploded into a collection of sparklers. The kind the kids loved to run around with on the Fourth of July. Giggling and laughing in half-joy, half-terror: caught up in the ecstasy of the celebration, but at the same time dreadfully afraid of being burnt. Little hands held as far from little bodies as possible. Little mouths wrinkled in fear-smiles. Laughter that tilted into ranges that blurred with hysteria. When you were a child, the lines between euphoria and panic could disappear in an instant.

But they loved the things. Loved the sparklers that Ken now saw everywhere in his eyes, in his mind.

Especially Derek.

Have to buy extra for him this year.

But he's dead, isn't he?

Another thud. Ken felt wetness on the back of his neck. Warmth flowing down his skin.

Stop hitting me.

Third concussion. Or is it my fourth?

What's the world record for noggin knocks?

Someone call Guiness!

His thoughts were just so much loose change rattling in his skull. But he was suddenly aware that he was no longer lighter than himself. The thing that had been pulling him upward had stopped yanking at him.

In fact... he turned his head. Slowly. It took longer than it should have. His neck creaked like a rusty hinge.

He was out of the elevator.

Everything was illuminated in flickering half-shadows. Ken couldn't tell if that was because something was wrong with Christian's light –

(*Wait, is his name Christian or Christopher? Or just Chris? What's his name again? Derek?*)

– or with his own vision. Maybe both. Perhaps all three.

Three? What three? Aren't there more of us? Not just three? Derek, Liz, Hope?

Hope isn't one of us.

You're losing it, Ken.

Everything seemed disjointed. Separated. But he managed to make out Buck through the gap in the elevator doors and through the clouds of acid-smoke that poured out of the cab. The big man – more a silhouette than a featured figure – threw something round behind him –

(*It's a head where did he get a head why isn't he wearing his head?*)

– and then leaped for the gap.

Behind Buck, bright streams of black light poured down. A sound like bacon frying chittered into the air.

"Move!" someone shouted.

It's the cowboy man. The killer man.

Buck made it to the doors. Pushed himself into the gap.

The elevator started to fall out from under his back foot.

Metal pinged. Popped.

Buck's face slackened. He looked... relieved. Like he'd been hoping for this.

And the elevator fell out from beneath him.

74

Ken lurched at Buck. His vision had strange black spots in it now, and he couldn't see much of what he was doing, but he saw the elevator fall, and saw the big man's face. Saw that the man wanted to fall, wanted to die.

Ken grabbed him. Pulled him forward, yanked him the rest of the way into the hall at the same instant the elevator's overstressed and acid-eroded cables and brakes finally gave up their fight with gravity. The entire apparatus fell, and Ken caught a glimpse of what seemed like hundreds of zombies crawling over the top of the elevator car, vomiting that darkly glowing acid and then reaching for the gap in the outer doors as they plunged past.

Then gone.

Buck was weeping. Sobbing and saying, "Shoulda let me fall, shoulda let me fall," over and over.

Ken stared at him dumbly. He didn't know what was happening. His thoughts still tumbled in a free-fall that matched that of the elevator.

A crash sounded from the elevator shaft, and shrieking cries echoed up the chimney-like structure.

"Did you hit me?" said Ken. He didn't intend it as a way of snapping Buck out of his litany of self-pity, he was far too frazzled and confused himself to do something like that. Still, Buck stopped his recitation and nodded. He was half atop Ken again, and Ken thought, We've got to stop meeting like this.

Aloud, he said, "Why?"

"I wasn't trying to," said Buck. "I was trying to get that thing to let go of you."

"Oh."

"I hit you with the head."

That didn't make sense for a second. Then Ken understood. "With the zombie head?"

Buck nodded. "It wouldn't let go when I hit it, so I figured...." He shrugged.

Ken laughed. The laughter hurt his head. And his back and his ribs and everything else below his hairline. But he couldn't stop.

Until his daughter started shrieking.

75

At first Ken actually got excited when he heard the sound. Because it was the sound of a baby crying.

Liz.

But when he scrambled to his feet, he saw Maggie. Saw Liz still dangling like a lifeless ragdoll from the carrier. The toddler's head slumped forward, her beautiful blond hair obscuring her face.

She's dying.

Ken ignored that thought. Even though he knew it was more than likely. Toddlers didn't stay unconscious for this long through this much unless there was something seriously wrong with them.

Still, he forced himself to focus on something else. On the source of the shriek that was not Liz. Was not a toddler screaming in pain and confusion upon waking to a world turned inside out.

No, it was Hope. The seven-year-old was standing between Maggie and Ken, rigid as a steel bar, fists clenched at her sides. Her face was turned up, her mouth opened.

And she screamed.

Ken had never heard Hope scream like that before. She was a daredevil, always the first one on the playground, always the first one to try a new toy... and so always the first one to fall and the first one to get hurt. But even with the bumps and bruises and cuts and scrapes, he had never heard her sound like this. She sounded like every atom of her body was being ripped away, one at a time, in a torture so horrific that no one would ever understand it.

Then she fell. The strength visibly fled from her limbs, and where every muscle had been clenched a moment before, now she transformed to a jumble of loose bones and skin.

"Hope!" shouted Maggie.

Aaron and Christopher were both near Ken's daughter, one on each side of her. Both moved for her, but the cowboy reached her first. He caught the little girl before she fell, wrapping her up in his good arm.

"Let me," said Christopher.

"No," said Aaron. "I got her."

"Really?" said Christopher. He rolled his eyes. "You got one good arm, man."

"I'm fine."

Something moved past Ken. It took a moment for him to realize it was Buck. The big man took Hope from Aaron without a word, cradling her gently in his arms.

He looked different holding her. Not the petulant, entitled ass he had seemed to be at first. Not the self-pitying man of a moment before.

He seemed whole. Like he was holding not merely a little girl, but the only thing tethering him to life. Not survival, but *life*. Two different things, Ken knew.

"We should go," said Buck. His voice was strange, and Ken wondered what was happening. Not just to Buck, but to all of them. The world had changed, and the change had not escaped them.

What are we?

"Maybe I –" Maggie began. She took a step toward the man.

"Let him," said Ken. He felt woozy, and put a hand to his neck. It came back red. Sticky. He wanted to vomit. He leaned against a wall that was painted white and had red streaks across it. Like everything else, it was dirty and bloodied.

He felt an arm slip under his. Knew it was Dorcas.

"Where to?" she said.

Why are you asking me?

He blinked. Everyone was looking at him. Everyone but Maggie, who was staring at Buck like she expected him to run off with Hope at any second.

Ken wiped his mouth. He needed to drink something. He was thirsty.

His fingers came up red as well. He hoped it was just a bloody cheek, and not internal bleeding.

More screams came from inside the elevator shaft. Closer. They were climbing back up.

"Let's go," he said.

He pushed away from the wall.

Dorcas had to help him.

76

"Where now?" asked Christopher. Ken waited for someone to answer, then realized with a start that they were looking at him.

Waiting for him.

He didn't know why. Maybe because he was from Boise? But so was Christopher.

Because he had family? That didn't make much sense.

Regardless, they waited. And he hated it. He hated that suddenly he had more than just a daughter in a coma and another who wanted to go to the monsters and a wife who hated him for losing their son to worry about.

Now he was responsible for *everyone*? When had that happened?

He didn't have time to figure it out, or time to argue about the fairness of it. He looked around. They were in another hallway, and one that didn't look familiar. He'd never been here before. He'd been in the upper floors of the building – though the floors had been several blocks over at the time – but he had no idea if the layout was the same or not.

He decided to assume they were.

"Left."

They moved. Christopher took point, leading the way with his light, sweeping it left and right. Buck and Maggie followed, each holding a silent child.

Ken and Dorcas limped behind them.

Aaron brought up the rear. Ken saw the older man sag for a moment, and wondered how badly *he* was hurting. But then the dangerous look returned to the cowboy's eyes and Ken knew that anything – man, beast, or monster – that came upon Aaron in the next few minutes would likely regret the move.

The corridor was deserted. Doors lined the way, and papers littered the floor where they had fallen from several billboards on the walls. Probably advertising local businesses and clothing drives and the upcoming "Fill the Boot" drive where local firefighters stood in the streets with empty boots asking for donations for burn victims.

No more of those. Plenty of victims, but the first responders were gone. Dead or themselves converted to the scourge that had swept the earth nearly clean of human life.

It was a marvel that this place was even standing. The top of the building had been blown clean off by a combination of a collision with a stealth fighter and exploding ordnance, and Ken figured it wouldn't take a whole lot more for the whole place to come down around their ears.

Everyone else seemed to be thinking the same thing. No one spoke. It felt like they weren't in a building, but in a hole deep underground. The kind of place where touching the wrong thing would cause a subterranean landslide.

He and Dorcas were falling behind the others. Ken realized it at the same moment he felt a hand at his back, gently urging him to greater speed.

"I don't know if he can," said Dorcas, responding to Aaron's unspoken exhortation.

"Gotta," said Aaron.

And Ken knew why. He could hear it, too. Could hear the things coming out of the elevator shaft in the darkness behind them.

Some of them must have perished in the fall. Or if not perished, then at least been damaged beyond the ability to climb back up. Laying at the bottom of the shaft, their broken bodies intertwined with the wreckage and cables.

But some had made it up. More than some.

It sounded like a lot.

77

"Here!"

Ken heard Buck shout, then saw the big man dart to the side. A moment later Christopher wheeled around and followed. So did Maggie.

Ken moved through the open doorway the rest of them had disappeared through, partially of his own volition and partially because Dorcas more or less pushed him through. He didn't know what would happen if she let go of him, but suspected he'd just fall and lay there. Maybe twitch a bit if he was lucky.

Once inside the door, everything disappeared. Literally. There was no trace of Buck or Maggie or Christopher or the kids. No trace of anything at all, for that matter. No office, no floor, no nothing. Just empty space before them, dimly lit from somewhere below.

It took a moment for Ken to refocus, to crane his neck down, each vertebra popping and screaming in protest as he did so. He felt something trickling on his lip and figured his nose was bleeding as well.

Can't keep this up.

Not much choice.

Sure, keep telling yourself that, Ken.

He finally saw the floor. It had collapsed a few feet past the doorway, falling away at a forty-five degree angle and ending in a pile of rubble on the level below.

At the bottom of the ramp, Maggie was being helped to her feet by Buck and Christopher. Buck was still holding Hope, and Liz sagged from her carrier, arms and legs limp and lifeless-seeming. It was clear that they had all slid down, and just as clear that this was the best way to make their way one floor closer to freedom from this building.

"Come on!" shouted Buck.

"You're nuts," said Dorcas. Ken couldn't tell if she was talking to him or Buck or herself.

"Not much choice," he said.

A grunt sounded behind them. Aaron. He squeezed into the small area of the floor that still remained intact and then slammed the door shut. "Go," he spat.

Dorcas sighed. She sounded beyond tired. Weary. Losing hope.

How much longer before we just stop? Before dying becomes preferable?

But that wasn't really the question. If death had been the stake, then Ken suspected they would have given up long before this. It wasn't just death, though. It was whatever waited at the end of a bite. Whatever cross between madness and oblivion would claim them.

Not just death, but damnation.

Dorcas helped Ken lower himself to a seated position, then sat behind him, her arms clasped around him and supporting most of his weight. He remembered doing this with Liz and Hope and Derek, all of them sitting in a long train on the slide at the local park, sliding down and laughing and then laughing harder when their combined mass inevitably caused them to stall halfway down. "Daddy's Choo-choo" they called it.

"Choo-choo time," he muttered. Tears came to his eyes. Derek would never ride the slide again. Not even if they had playgrounds in Heaven. Because he *hadn't* simply died. Nothing so kind. Nothing so merciful.

Ken thought he might lose it. He had seen his own students pull each others' guts apart, had cut his own fingers off to survive, had somehow waded through a city full of the living dead. And now he was going to be done in by the memory of a little boy laughing as he went down a slide.

"What?" said Dorcas. She glanced back at the door with eyes clearly expecting it to be flung open at any moment.

"Nothing." Ken leaned forward. Tilting into darkness, but away from memory.

He slid down the broken floor. Dorcas came with him. He moved faster than he expected – a lot faster than the green plastic slide at the park – and started to panic when he realized he was going to roll off the edge of the floor and into a pile of broken shelving that featured several stake-like pieces of wood and metal.

Christopher snagged him, reaching out and stopping his forward momentum with a low, "Oof." A similar noise nearby indicated that Buck and Maggie had stopped Dorcas.

Christopher helped Ken to his feet as Aaron came sliding down. The cowboy somehow ended the slide on his feet, not needing any help but seeming to just step off and start walking forward, gesturing for the others to follow.

Dorcas resumed her position under Ken's arm. He glanced at Maggie as she did so, wondering – hoping – if his wife would try to take the older woman's place.

Maggie didn't. She didn't even look at him.

Just turned her back and followed Aaron as he picked his way through the rubble.

78

This room was a large interior room of the building. No outside windows, so the only illumination was still Christopher's light. A light that did little to brighten, and less to cheer. It served to highlight large objects in their path, but not much else.

Aaron was still in the lead, but Christopher was right beside him. Buck and Maggie followed them, the kids in their arms.

And Dorcas and Ken were left in back. With the noises.

At first Ken thought that the things had found them already. Strange sounds assaulted him at every step. And every time he heard something it registered as more than noise. It was a blow to the base of his spine, a pounding that ran the length of his already-pained left leg, then up to his back and through to the bottom of his skull before rattling around in his head like a bell clapper.

"What's wrong with you?" Dorcas whispered, and Ken realized his entire face had pulled tight as a miser's purse string, his mouth puckered and his jaw clenched. He tried to relax, but then heard another noise and his muscles contracted of their own accord.

"The noise," he said.

Dorcas kept moving forward, but cocked her head. "I don't hear anything."

Ken gritted his teeth as the sound – now a combination of the zombies' growl, sheet metal bending, and nails scraping plates – sounded again. "You're not hearing that?" he said.

Dorcas shook her head. Her expression changed. And suddenly she didn't look like the friendly, selfless woman who had risked herself time and again for Ken and the others. Now she looked like one of *them*. The skin seemed to fall from her flesh, the bones peeked out from her cheeks.

"What?"

Ken blinked. The zombie was gone. Dorcas was back. Back and she wasn't hearing what he was hearing.

"Dorcas, I think I'm in trouble," he whispered. His feet felt funny, too. He looked down and realized that he was leaving a steady trail of blood behind him, though he couldn't tell what part of him it was coming from.

"Guys," Dorcas whispered. "Guys!" Ken sensed rather than saw the halt of the parade of survivors. "We need to stop."

Footsteps. Ken felt arms around him, displacing Dorcas' arm and lifting him a bit higher than she had done. "Can't," said a voice. Ken recognized it as Aaron. But he couldn't actually see the cowboy. Everything seemed far too dark.

"Where's the light?" Ken said. "Why'd Chris turn off the light?" His voice sounded slurred and distant.

"Shit," said someone else. And Ken had no idea who had spoken. "What's wrong with him?"

"What do you think?"

Ken felt his body pulled forward, moved along by the hands that held him up, the arms that held him aloft.

He heard the sounds again. And this time knew it wasn't just his injury-addled mind. Because someone cursed, and someone else said, "They found the door."

79

Ken's vision went from a mixture of sparklers-and-hallucinations to sparklers-and-globby-black-things.

A moment later the globby black things killed the sparklers. All was dark.

He could feel himself being dragged. Could hear sounds.

Growls. The distant – but rapidly approaching – noises of the horde.

Voices.

"Spread out. Look for it." Sounded like Aaron.

"You kidding? What are the chances it'll –" An unfamiliar voice. But whining a bit, so probably Buck.

"With all the different allergies people have, almost one in ten people need it or have a family member that does." Aaron, farther away.

"Hold on, Ken." A voice in his ear. Whispering. Dorcas. Or no, not Dorcas. Someone else. Who was that?

"Still bad odds." Buck's grumble.

"Add in the mothers who keep one for their kids, the odds go up."

"Still, I –"

"Found one!"

"Just like I flrpp mrp mpt tpp."

Even the sounds melted into one another.

Ken felt alone.

So this is what it feels like to die.

"Hold on."

This voice was clearer. Understandable. And he could place it now. Not Dorcas.

Maggie. Telling him not to die. That he mattered to her.

He couldn't smile. Couldn't move a muscle. So he probably *was* dying.

But he felt better, just the same.

Everything disappeared.

80

Something bit him. A stinging pinch on his outer thigh that rapidly shifted from discomfort to agony.

They found us!

Ken wanted to scream, but couldn't. His jaw locked up

–

(*This is what it feels like to become one of them.*)

– and he was paralyzed by terror, pain, and sorrow. The last because he knew the others must be dead. There was no way they would have left him to the zombies. So if he was being bitten, was changing, then they were all gone.

Dorcas, Aaron, Christopher. Even Buck.

And Maggie. Liz. Hope.

Something bit his other leg.

The paralysis broke. Ken's heart rate seemed to quadruple, and he surged upward, swinging his arms at whatever was eating him.

His right fist connected with something that was both soft and hard. The thing popped, crackled.

"OW! *Seriously?*"

Ken blinked. The dark blobbies were floating away, trailing the last of the July Fourth sparklers in their wake, leaving behind something that resembled normal vision. Revealing not the expected monsters chomping on his legs, but….

"Christopher?"

The young man was holding his nose, which was spurting blood all over the front of his previously unmarked shirt. "You broge by dose," he said.

Ken looked down. His right fist was still clenched. It ached. Probably less than Christopher's nose ached, but enough to verify the young man's claim.

Aaron was kneeling at Ken's right. Grinning at Ken, then at Christopher. "You were too pretty anyway," said the cowboy.

The younger man mumbled something that sounded like "Fug oo," but probably wasn't. Aaron chuckled.

Ken blinked. Wiped away a sheet of sweat that had appeared on his forehead. His hand shook as though the movement was a bit too fine for it. His motor control seemed off.

"What... what happened?" said Ken.

Aaron plucked something off the floor by Christopher. Held it in front of Ken, along with a match he held in his own hand. "EpiPens," said the cowboy.

"Wha?" Ken wasn't processing this.

"The stuff people use for bee stings and peanut allergies. It's basically just a shot of adrenaline." Aaron stood. Held out a hand to Ken. He took it and, surprisingly, managed to stand. "You, sir, are banged up pretty bad. But we bought you some time."

A scream sounded. Aaron looked up as though trying to pinpoint the source.

Something hit Ken. Wrapped itself around him like a constrictor. He almost panicked, almost swung at the thing. His nerves were pulled tighter than ukulele strings.

It was only at the last second that he recognized the strange shape as that of his wife. With Liz in front of her, between them as she held to him.

"What's happening?" she sobbed.

He put his arms around her. And for a moment the world was fine again. For just a second, the space *between* seconds, he felt alive, felt right.

He had lost Derek.

Liz was unconscious.

Hope was... different.

But his wife still loved him. That was something.

"End of the world, baby," he said. He kissed her hair. It smelled awful. Sweat and blood and the webbing she had been wrapped in and a thousand other things, none of them pleasant. But it was Maggie and he just wanted to drink her in.

"Love this, really," said Buck. Ken looked over. The big man was still holding Hope, thrown over his shoulder in a rough fireman's carry. "But we gotta get outta here."

Ken nodded. He drew Maggie back. Kissed her on her lips, full-on. Not passionate, exactly, but not the "honey-I'm-leaving-for-work" peck either. A real kiss. He needed her to know what she meant to him. What it would mean to him if something happened to her.

He saw her eyes.

Saw that she understood.

And then realized that someone else was staring at him.

Liz.

The two-year-old hadn't opened her eyes through all this. Now her eyes were open, and staring at him in a way that sent shivers not just through Ken's spine, but through his soul.

He tried to convince himself that it was all right. This was good. She was *awake*.

Ken realized that everyone had stopped moving. Maggie was staring at the toddler, watching her with excitement. And he couldn't begin to imagine what it must have been like for her to see her daughter hanging comatose for all this time.

The entire world seemed silent.

Liz smiled.

And Ken's stomach seemed to fall into his legs. It wasn't the adrenaline surging through his body, either. He knew about adrenaline; knew it was a stop-gap and that he maybe had an hour before he crashed again and was back to being nothing more than a bleeding burden on the group. But it wasn't that. It wasn't his injuries.

It was the smile. Not the smile of an infant. Not the smile of his Lizzy.

She spoke. The same high-pitched toddler voice, but it wasn't "Lizzy go now" or even his favorite "Daddy kisses." She looked at each person in the company, even straining her neck to look at Maggie, then said in a cold voice, "You are not family. You are renegades."

And then Liz started to scream. Her body contorted in seizure spasms, the movements of someone who has not only lost all control, but who never had it in the first place.

Ken looked at Maggie. She was staring at her daughter in horror, trying to hold the baby's flailing limbs, trying to keep her from hurting herself.

Growling came from above them. The pounding of feet on the ceiling.

"Good God," said Buck. "She called them. She called them to us."

Ken looked at the man and wanted to scream that it wasn't true, wanted to shriek at him and punch him into submission because how *dare* he say such a thing about Ken's baby?

But he didn't.

It *was* true.

The monsters were among them.

END OF BOOK TWO
THE SAGA WILL CONTINUE IN BOOK THREE
THE COLONY: DESCENT

ABOUT THE AUTHOR

Michaelbrent Collings is an award-winning screenwriter and novelist. He has written numerous bestselling horror, thriller, sci-fi, and fantasy novels, including *Strangers, Darkbound, Apparition, The Haunted, Hooked: A True Faerie Tale,* and the bestselling YA series *The Billy Saga.* Follow him on Facebook (at facebook.com/MichaelbrentCollings) or on Twitter @mbcollings.

And if you liked *The Colony: Renegades*, please leave a review on your favorite book review site... and tell your friends!

Made in the USA
San Bernardino, CA
02 May 2014